I0600532

We Must Kill Toni

A Comedy

by Ian Stuart Black

A SAMUEL FRENCH ACTING EDITION

SAMUEL FRENCH

FOUNDED 1830

New York Hollywood London Toronto

SAMUELFRENCH.COM

WE MUST KILL TONI was first presented in London at the "Q Theatre," London, on April 17, 1951, with the following cast of characters:

DOUGLAS OBERON .... *Guy Rolfe*

FRANCIS OBERON .... *John Justin*

HARRIS .... *Noel Howlitt*

MISS RICHARDS .... *Nita Moyce*

TONI OBERON .... *Eileen Moore*

The play produced by Willard Stoker

The action of the play takes place in an old English country mansion during the first few weeks of spring.

ACT I

SCENE 1: Evening.
SCENE 2: The following morning.

ACT II

SCENE 1: Evening, a few days later.
SCENE 2: The following afternoon.

ACT III

That evening.

PREFACE FOR PRODUCERS

There will come a time during rehearsals, when the actress playing Toni will ask her producer to what extent she is to let the audience know she is aware of the sinister plots against her. At what point is she to take the audience into her confidence? There are several possible answers, but my feeling is that Toni never puts all her cards on the table; and never takes anyone completely into her confidence—not even Harris. She carries her air of innocence right to the end, even while preparing her most diabolical counter-plot.

Toni, indeed, never comes out of the frame around her; nor do her cousins. Douglas and Francis live entirely in a world of their own, and obey its laws. The real world lies on the other side of their feudal village, and it is a tiresome irrelevancy. These three central characters must be played with a style and control not generally necessary in more realistic comedies.

Much of the amusement in this play grows out of the threatened dangers. It is very important to make these appear real dangers. The two men must always intend to carry out their plans—and at no time does anyone on the stage ever indicate that a situation is amusing. To the Oberon family this is not a comedy, but a life or death struggle—with rapiers, and no mercy.

The dialogue is often not conventional speech. It requires a precision, almost a rhythm, if its artificial quality is to be obvious. And this is important, as you must let your audience know they are now in a world as artificial as Alice's "Wonderland." Once they accept this, then murder—or even marriage—can become amusing.

As regards casting, it must be remembered that for all her obvious feminine charm, Toni is the most intelligent Oberon. She has brains behind those guileless eyes. Unless the actress can convince her audience in Act II, Scene 2, that she is playing a dangerous and intricate game with great cunning, then the tea-party scene will go for little—and the end of the play develops from this important scene. We must be persuaded that Toni is capable of fighting and defeating her two cousins; then the audience should follow her moves with understanding and, let us hope, approval.

This is a play without a villain. The two men should be acted with elegance and charm. Douglas is the more brutal, and at times he over-simplifies the situation. He is prepared to act first and think afterwards—if thinking is absolutely necessary. Francis is more gentle and subtle, and perhaps more ruthless. As Douglas and the direct approach to murder gradually fail, Francis and the intelligent approach take more control. But the main point is that both Francis and Douglas should be deep in the affections of the audience by the end of the play. They are a couple of aristocrats left over from the French Revolution, and somehow uncontaminated by our modern way of life. Technically they must act together as a unit. Their dialogue, their discussions, their plans, must all be taken at a good tempo. They should bounce the ball of conversation backwards and forwards rapidly to each other. Their scenes should bubble.

Next on our list is Harris. Harris is not an old man. He is an "ageless" man. Logically he must be about 102, but we ignore the last thirty years. He is an abstraction, distilled from all the faithful retainers that ever were. (Except, of course, that Harris is not faithful.) He dates back to the first Oberons; but he carries his age well. Harris is devoted to the two men. He would save them if he could. But he cannot do that without stepping outside the conventions, without becoming real; and that is unthinkable! Harris transfers his devotion to Toni as he recognises that the strength of the Oberon family lies in her, rather than in the men. How right and proper.

Miss Richards, that intrusion from a busy, vulgar world, completes the cast. It is a part which can be played in several ways; with a smart, professional simplicity; with a certain gushing over-enthusiasm; with an inane lack of comprehension. Whichever way it is played, however, it must be done with speed, keeping on a completely different tone from the Oberons, and drawing no undue attention to itself. That is a good deal to ask of any actress.

IAN STUART BLACK

We Must Kill Toni

ACT I

SCENE 1

There is only one set in this play. It is the central room of a very old mansion. It dates back to mediaeval times, but there have been additions and alterations made to it by every generation since then. The main features are a door off to the entrance hall, a staircase leading upstairs, a cellar opening leading downstairs, and a corridor leading to servant's quarters and to the rest of the house. Along this corridor, just off-stage and unseen, is a heavy door which can be bolted in the last act. The positions used in this production are as follows: The door leading to the entrance hall and garden is in the corner, U. R., *at a slight angle. It is on a landing, raised a step above the level of the rest of the room. This landing is shared with the staircase, which runs along the back of the stage,* U. C., *the foot of the stairs turning at an angle into the room,* U. R. *In this way, actors coming down stairs, and in from the front door, meet on the landing.* D. R. *is an ancient, open fireplace. There is a chair above it, and a stool below. In the first and last scenes of the play, the sofa is against the back wall,* C. *It is near the fireplace* D. R. *for Act I, Scene 2, and for all Act II. The cellar opening is* U. S., *slightly* L. *of* C. D. S. *from it is the dining-table, flanked by chairs. This table is moved up to take the place of the sofa against the wall,* U. C., *in the three scenes when the sofa is by the fireplace. On the* L. *side of the stage is an arch over the corridor, which leads off to* HARRIS'S *door and the rest of the house. Above it is the sideboard,*

7

*against the wall. The room is decorated with ancient
weapons, and a forbidding ancient portrait or two.
On the landing, above the stairs, is a stained-glass
window, through which the moon shines in Act II,
when the other lights are out.*

As the curtain goes up on Act I, we see FRANCIS *and*
DOUGLAS OBERON, *two very elegant men, seated over
the remnants of dinner. They are not young men,
yet still in their thirties. It is hard to say which is
the elder. They are distinguished, one from the other,
by their different approach to a common problem.*
DOUGLAS *is for solving everything with a slash of
the knife;* FRANCIS *hopes to achieve more by guile.
Both are equally dangerous, equally unscrupulous.
They have been discussing something for some time,
and are meditating over it as the curtain goes up.*

DOUGLAS. (*At* R. *of table.*) Murder or marriage?

(*Enter* HARRIS D. L. *with drinks. He is an old man, a
"timeless" old man.*)

HARRIS. (L. *of table.*) Port, sir?
FRANCIS. Brandy.
HARRIS. (*To* DOUGLAS.) Brandy, sir?
DOUGLAS. Port. (HARRIS *pours the drinks and goes
out* D. L.)
FRANCIS. Marriage or murder . . . an intriguing alter-
native.
DOUGLAS. Murder is conclusive.
FRANCIS. Marriage can be final.
DOUGLAS. But murder is tidier.
FRANCIS. Marriage is less dangerous.
DOUGLAS. H'm. (*They drink.*) What's it to be? Mar-
riage?
FRANCIS. You think murder?
DOUGLAS. It has certain advantages.
FRANCIS. And disadvantages, too.

DOUGLAS. It gets her out of the way.

FRANCIS. Irreparably so.

DOUGLAS. Perhaps you're right.

FRANCIS. There's a great deal in what you say. H'm. (*They drink.*) Very fine brandy.

DOUGLAS. Excellent port. You see it's like this. If she's murdered, the episode is over and done with, once and for all. If we marry her, this state of affairs will go on for ever.

FRANCIS. But the risks, my dear Douglas. The attendant risks to murder nowadays. Do you think it advisable?

DOUGLAS. Isn't marriage also said to be a risk?

FRANCIS. Yes, but one more easily negotiated than murder.

DOUGLAS. Something could surely be devised.

FRANCIS. Suspicion would be immediate. Motives are so obvious. If the girl dies we inherit her money. It's entailed. It returns to the estate.

DOUGLAS. But motives are insufficient to convict a man, Francis.

FRANCIS. Motives are sufficient to wind up a case, Douglas.

DOUGLAS. Quite a dilemma.

FRANCIS. Surely in a case like this, it's wisest to be guided by the past? (*Gets up, walks to bookshelf, and takes out ancient well-worn book. Goes back to table with it. Sits.*)

DOUGLAS. I quite agree. Our fathers faced this problem a hundred times. How was it solved?

FRANCIS. The nineteenth century mostly married the girl. (*Looking up from book.*)

DOUGLAS. That was before the emancipation of women. It won't work now. Earlier centuries were all for murder. (*He, too, points to book as authority.*)

FRANCIS. With small success.

DOUGLAS. With great success.

FRANCIS. (*Pushing book, open at certain page, across to* DOUGLAS.) Ancestor Ethelred, for example, in 1256.

The family history tells us that he chose murder, but tripped into the molten lead himself.

DOUGLAS. (*Using book to prove his point as well.*) But, Francis, he was an exception. You have forgotten Arthur, and Egbert, and Constantine Oberon; pages eighty-two to ninety-eight: three generations of inspired assassinations, an accident while riding, a stray arrow at a hawking party, a pricked finger on a rusty spindle. They had ·no difficulty in dispatching the females who stood between them and their mother's lands. (*He slams book shut with finality.*)

FRANCIS. Things were much eaiser in the olden days.

DOUGLAS. Nonsense! The house is still full of their swords and battle-axes; some still as sharp. (*Waving hand airily at weapons which decorate room.*)

FRANCIS. I meant it was easier to carry it off.

DOUGLAS. I suppose so.

FRANCIS. Just for the sake of argument, let us consider marriage. Marry the girl, and the estate at least remains in the family.

DOUGLAS. But she will have her legal rights. She will have her advisers. She will be always here, there, and in the way.

FRANCIS. But it would be a compromise which would assure us the spoils.

DOUGLAS. Would it not be a constant danger to have her always present, the final word of authority: and we the creatures of her capricious whims?

FRANCIS. Not if she is married. (*They both are arguing the point with politeness but great eagerness.*)

DOUGLAS. Ultimately, she will discover this deception.

FRANCIS. We must not let her.

DOUGLAS. That would involve an eternal endeavour.

FRANCIS. Nothing is achieved without endeavour.

DOUGLAS. Then let our endeavour be quick, sharp, accurate and to the heart; not a life-sentence of humble dependency.

FRANCIS. My dear Douglas, you are too impetuous

with your paper knife. Sergeant X will find the implement: Inspector Y carefully examine the ornate handle and the ivory blade: Z will interpret the marks, the smudges and the stains. My dear Douglas.

DOUGLAS. And you, my dear Francis, are too dilatory, Solicitor A will hear the details: Barrister B state the case: and C will grant the decree nisi.

FRANCIS. Murder will out.

DOUGLAS. Marriage will reveal the man.

FRANCIS. Let us begin at least with caution; not take a step that's irrevocable.

DOUGLAS. Very well, I agree to marriage.

FRANCIS. You are most conciliatory, but I think you will find you are well advised.

DOUGLAS. I have no doubt. Now, what of the lady? Her precise relationship to us? Her age? Her looks, breeding, education? These are points which I fancy might profitably be discussed.

FRANCIS. My dear Douglas, we have been over this a dozen times already.

DOUGLAS. There is no harm in a further summary of so important an issue. She is the nearest female relative to our late lamented great-grandmother. What more does that lawyer's letter tell us? (*Picks up letter from table between them, with distaste.*)

FRANCIS. Nothing, only that she has now reached the stipulated age at which she inherits our estates.

DOUGLAS. And straightway she is swooping on her prey?

FRANCIS. So it would seem.

DOUGLAS. Too avaricious for the ideal wife. Do you suppose she has great beauty to compensate?

FRANCIS. Her colouring, so I am told, is faded. Her hair straw-like in texture, mousy coloured. Her features are insignificant, and her figure flat.

DOUGLAS. My dear fellow, perhaps after all, murder . . .

FRANCIS. Her education has been neglected by several

schools for gentlewomen. Yet she has one saving grace. Her breeding, which, in so far as it is derivative from our own stock, is impeccable.

DOUGLAS. Her looks? Just how plain is she?

FRANCIS. There you have me. (*Taking photographs from wallet.*) A few photographs of an angular school-girl going through the difficult stages of the irregular verbs are of little assistance; more recently, a newspaper clipping which shows her behind a soup-spoon at a hunt ball. The glossy magazines have her under a hat at Ascot, beneath a mink at the opera, disguised at the Carnival of Flowers. (*Hands each to* DOUGLAS, *as he discusses them.*)

DOUGLAS. (*Looking at photos.*) The flowers are very pretty . . . and the mink is real.

FRANCIS. Her wealth is sufficient to engulf a whole jungle of minks.

DOUGLAS. (*Handing back photos.*) And it is into such coffers that our poor pittance is poured! All due to a wicked system devised by ancient royalty, afraid to trust their sons, or conscious of their daughters' ineligibility amongst princes.

FRANCIS. Be that as it may, it is our burden. We must bear it or break it.

DOUGLAS. If marriage will break it, all well and good. When do you propose to marry the girl?

FRANCIS. I, brother?

DOUGLAS. Yes, brother.

FRANCIS. Not I, brother. I had planned for you to marry her.

DOUGLAS. Oh, no, my plan was murder. I'm responsible for that. If we have murder I'll attend to it, but now we have marriage. That is your concern.

FRANCIS. But I have not your looks, your figure, your fascination for women.

DOUGLAS. Nor have I your grace, your height, your most charming manners. I repeat, it is your plan. You must marry the girl. (FRANCIS *reflects—a moment's pause.*)

FRANCIS. On reconsidering the scheme in the light of further information, and taking into consideration all its varying aspects, I feel inclined to think that there is something to be said for your original idea.

DOUGLAS. You do?

FRANCIS. I agree to murder.

DOUGLAS. You are very conciliatory, but I think you will find you are well advised.

FRANCIS. I have no doubt. But what of the method? The precise form of murder? The weapon? The time, the place, the approach? These are points we might very well discuss.

DOUGLAS. I have given it some thought.

FRANCIS. Have you reached a decision?

DOUGLAS. I have not. (*Takes walnuts from silver nut dish on table.*) Let us examine the methods of the past. Hanging, burning and knifing were numerous in Tudor times. Poison and strangulation have always been popular. Burying alive had quite a vogue in Queen Anne's day. Shooting is modern, and nuclear explosion as yet untried. (*Cracks nuts.*)

FRANCIS. Nothing too noisy.

DOUGLAS. Perhaps not.

FRANCIS. Nor too complicated. A muffled strangulation might fit the bill.

DOUGLAS. Strangulation would do nicely.

FRANCIS. There's something to be said for hanging, burning, or burying alive, if they can be made to look like an accident.

DOUGLAS. A very important point, for we must cover our tracks. I have considered using the advantages we have at hand . . . this very old building. After all, if she inherits our ancestral home, ought she not to lay her bones at rest here? What could be more fitting than the old wine cellar?

FRANCIS. Amongst the vats and barrels?

DOUGLAS. Exactly. Lean on a crumbling beam: step on a treacherous board. Alas! So sad! So sudden! So unpremeditated! Nothing so deadly fatal as a ton of masonry.

FRANCIS. An excellent idea. And if it fails, we still have choice enough before us to assure success before the visit ends.

DOUGLAS. We have indeed. The drop from the Jacobean Tower, a fall of eighty or ninety feet, with an odds-on chance of swift impaling.

FRANCIS. Yes, yes. I am sure you are right. Murder can be made to look like a careless step on the ruined tower, or an accident by an open fire. Why did I hesitate before? Marriage? I haven't a good word to say for it.

DOUGLAS. Yet it, too, was an excellent solution.

FRANCIS. It is good of you to say so, but I am now convinced. You have converted me . . . to murder.

DOUGLAS. I am happy to see it is so. Others might not have grasped the essentials quite so quickly. (HARRIS *enters* D. L. *to remove glasses.*) Harris, for example.

HARRIS. Sir? (*Moves in above table.*)

DOUGLAS. We are writing another story, Harris, my brother and I.

HARRIS. May I offer my congratulations, sir, and wish it more success than the last?

FRANCIS. This one will make money, Harris, never fear.

HARRIS. I rejoice to hear that, sir.

DOUGLAS. We would like to sound you on a point, Harris.

HARRIS. I am ready to be sounded, sir.

DOUGLAS. In our novel we have an alternative, and we are in a dilemma as to which is best. We have a girl, an intruder, a stranger, inherit the estates and wealth of an old family when the great-grandmother dies.

HARRIS. Indeed, sir?

DOUGLAS. The law of inheritance is matriarchal, and thus the property passes to this distant cousin, the last, the only, female heir. But for her existence all would have gone to the rightful owners, the present tenants, our heroes, two brilliant, charming, talented men.

HARRIS. This is something like your own case, sir.

DOUGLAS. Very like, very like. An artist is on safest ground when he takes his materials straight from life. To proceed: in an endeavour to protect their interest and retain their property, these two men are forced to dispense with this interloper in some way.

HARRIS. I see that, sir.

DOUGLAS. Two methods immediately jump to mind. Are they to neutralise her by marriage, or by murder?

HARRIS. You mean, electrocute her in her bath?

DOUGLAS. Thank you, Harris. We had not thought of that.

FRANCIS. Come, Harris, which is it to be? Marriage or murder?

HARRIS. In your story you mean, sir?

FRANCIS. Still in our story.

HARRIS. Then I'd plump for murder, sir.

DOUGLAS. Thank you, Harris. You may clear away. (HARRIS *takes the glasses and goes out* D. L.)

FRANCIS. Harris has put the black cap on for cousin Toni.

DOUGLAS. Encouraging to have the opinion of so thoughtful a man. I feel easier in my mind.

FRANCIS. With a light heart we can now proceed to plot the intricacies of cousin Toni's tragic end. Have you a scrap of paper?

DOUGLAS. The back of an envelope. (*Picking up envelope from table.*)

FRANCIS. We might polish off cousin Toni in so small a space. Let me see. We will head it "marriage or murder." That will be our code. Now, number one, cousin Toni; (*He is writing.*) number two, to forestall suspicion; number three, to make first attempt in the old wine cellar.

DOUGLAS. Precisely.

FRANCIS. How are we to get her there?

DOUGLAS. Force, guile, persuasion.

FRANCIS. I am crossing out force. I am putting a question mark over persuasion. Guile, I think. Guile. We must get her to go to the old cellar. We must make her provide us with alibis. We must . . . (*A BELL rings in the distance. The two men look inquiringly at each other.* HARRIS *enters* D. L. *and goes out* U. R., *into the front hall.*) What's the time?

DOUGLAS. It isn't the quarter.

FRANCIS. Could it be her?

DOUGLAS. It isn't possible. (HARRIS *re-enters* U. R.)

HARRIS. Excuse me, gentlemen. There is a journalist at the door.

DOUGLAS. At this time of night?

FRANCIS. We are expecting Miss Oberon, Harris. We cannot see anyone.

HARRIS. Yes, sir. I told her that.

DOUGLAS. Her?

HARRIS. It is a lady journalist—from London, sir. I believe it's about Miss Oberon. (*The brothers exchange glances.*)

DOUGLAS. Very well, Harris. Show her in. (*Exit* HARRIS U. R.)

FRANCIS. Don't forget, Douglas, we are delighted to see our cousin. We bear no resentment. We are glad to be quit of this ramshackle place. It's draughty. (HARRIS *enters* U. R.)

HARRIS. Miss Richards.

(HARRIS *stands to one side as* MISS RICHARDS *enters* U. R. *Only one half of her mind is ever centred on the situation before her: the other half is always in Fleet Street. Given a chance, she likes to rattle away to anyone who will listen to her. Thus, her interests and observations are only skin-deep. In spite of her professional charm she is still pleasant. She carries a camera. The two brothers rise politely.*)

MISS RICHARDS. Good evening. (MISS RICHARDS *stops abruptly and looks quickly, and with admiration, round the room.*) Oh! What a wonderful room. Is this to be

Miss Oberon's new home? (*Going* D. R. *a little.* HARRIS *crosses and goes out* D. L.)

FRANCIS. Good evening, madam. New is a relative term. This house was new eight hundred years ago.

MISS RICHARDS. How tactless of me. You must be the cousins. (*Moves further into room.*)

FRANCIS. As you so aptly put it.

MISS RICHARDS. Not that you are the least bit like Miss Oberon.

DOUGLAS. That much we've gathered from reports.

MISS RICHARDS. You've never met?

DOUGLAS. We are waiting for her now.

MISS RICHARDS. Oh, dear, I couldn't have called at a worse time.

FRANCIS. That's quite all right. Is there anything we can do?

MISS RICHARDS. I'm writing a little article about Miss Oberon. I hoped to have an interview. Perhaps a photo in the baronial hall.

FRANCIS. Oh, no; not there!

MISS RICHARDS. No?

DOUGLAS. We keep it locked up . . . ever since the skulls were found bricked up behind the wall.

MISS RICHARDS. Dear me! Could you suggest another place?

DOUGLAS. The east wing, Francis?

FRANCIS. What! With bloodstains on the floor?

DOUGLAS. The north wing?

FRANCIS. It's full of bats and owls.

DOUGLAS. Well, the guest-room then?

FRANCIS. Douglas! You can't put people into the guest-room after what happened there.

MISS RICHARDS. What happened there?

FRANCIS. Every family has its skeletons, Miss Richards. We do not like discussing ours.

DOUGLAS. I am sure you now appreciate how glad we are to leave this place.

MISS RICHARDS. You are?

DOUGLAS. Of course. We cannot wait to get away.

FRANCIS. We hope Miss Oberon is capable of standing up to things.

MISS RICHARDS. What sort of things? (*Steps into* C.)

FRANCIS. Living here seems to have a strange effect on some people, especially women. Perhaps the unusual power that they possess here goes to their head. (*Moving above table.*)

MISS RICHARDS. Indeed?

DOUGLAS. Our aunts, Clarissa and Isolda, for example. (*Crosses to fireplace.*)

MISS RICHARDS. What happened to your aunts?

FRANCIS. (*Above table.*) No sooner had they inherited the estate than, under the impression she was a fish, Clarissa dived into the lake.

DOUGLAS. Under the impression she was a witch, Isolda leapt from the chimney-stack.

MISS RICHARDS. Good gracious me!

DOUGLAS. Broomstick and all.

FRANCIS. Strange creatures, aunts.

(*Both men shake their heads sadly. They are one on either side of* MISS RICHARDS, *closing in for the last few speeches.* FRANCIS *now offers her a chair.*)

MISS RICHARDS. (*Protesting.*) But it's such a lovely old house. (*Sits* R. *of table.*) It doesn't seem to have upset you two in any way.

FRANCIS. Ah, no. We are perfectly normal. But it is different in our case. We were born here.

MISS RICHARDS. You have lived here all your life?

DOUGLAS. Yes.

MISS RICHARDS. You must have grown attached to it.

FRANCIS. It does exert a spell. Silly, isn't it? But one grows to be a part of it after twenty generations have built and bred here.

MISS RICHARDS. What a dreadful blow to have to leave!

DOUGLAS. Not at all, Miss Richards. We knew it would

happen sooner or later. We have had a lifetime to prepare for dispossession. (*He prowls* U. L.)

FRANCIS. We are quite anxious to give it up in spite of our attachment. We are waiting only to show our cousin round, before we say "good-bye."

MISS RICHARDS. What if Miss Oberon did not choose to stay?

DOUGLAS. Why should she not?

MISS RICHARDS. It's low lying. She may not find it healthy.

DOUGLAS. (*Moving* D. R. C.) Tell us, Miss Richards, is our cousin ever ill?

MISS RICHARDS. Not to my knowledge.

DOUGLAS. Suffer from sickness or disease?

MISS RICHARDS. Good gracious, no!

DOUGLAS. What's her resistance like? How strong is she?

(DOUGLAS *has taken out his pocket handkerchief. He now holds it tightly between his hands and twists it as he finishes the question.* FRANCIS *quickly covers him, as he does for all* DOUGLAS's *indiscretions.*)

FRANCIS. (*Crossing quickly between* DOUGLAS *and* MISS RICHARDS.) My brother meant, is she likely to be affected by the damp of this low lying area?

MISS RICHARDS. Oh, no. You won't have an invalid on your hands. Never fear.

FRANCIS. We are relieved to hear it.

MISS RICHARDS. How long does Miss Oberon intend to stay?

DOUGLAS. (*Crossing to fireplace.*) For ever—probably.

MISS RICHARDS. (*Rising from chair.*) Then perhaps I might call again and see her?

FRANCIS. Please do.

MISS RICHARDS. (*Crossing towards front door.*) Would to-morrow be all right? I'm staying in the village. When I have had my interview I can go back to town.

DOUGLAS. I am sure to-morrow will be all right.

MISS RICHARDS. Let's say round about noon?
DOUGLAS. At twelve o'clock.

(MISS RICHARDS *is preparing to go.* FRANCIS *detains her.*)

FRANCIS. We are so glad you called, Miss Richards. It's rather difficult preparing to meet Miss Oberon, knowing so little about her. I wondered if you could tell us, quite confidentially, what to expect.

MISS RICHARDS. I could, but I doubt if you'd believe me.

DOUGLAS. Why not?

MISS RICHARDS. She is so simple, naïve and innocent.

FRANCIS. Indeed?

MISS RICHARDS. I wouldn't like to be in her shoes, not for all her wealth: a tragic example of too much money and a sheltered life.

FRANCIS. Go on, Miss Richards. You interest us.

DOUGLAS. You fascinate us.

MISS RICHARDS. So strictly brought up, she has no knowledge of the world: so trusting, she is anyone's fool: and now, so rich she can never be sure of a friend.

FRANCIS. Miss Richards, we intend to change all that.

MISS RICHARDS. No one really cares for her.

FRANCIS. Douglas, we must prepare something very special for cousin Toni. Miss Richards, you know a great deal about her. What is her favourite dish?

MISS RICHARDS. Crêpe Suzette.

DOUGLAS. What is her favourite drink?

MISS RICHARDS. Bollinger '33.

DOUGLAS. Thank you. (*The CLOCK BELL tolls.* DOUGLAS *and* FRANCIS *are suddenly galvanised into activity.*) That's the quarter.

FRANCIS. Well, Miss Richards, we do not wish to appear impolite, but we expect Miss Oberon very shortly and should like to prepare to receive her.

(FRANCIS *rings the BELL for* HARRIS, *pulling a bell-rope on the wall.*)

MISS RICHARDS. I quite understand. Thank you so much. Do please let Miss Oberon know I shall call tomorrow.

DOUGLAS. Of course. Of course. (*Enter* HARRIS D. L.)

FRANCIS. Harris, Miss Richards is leaving.

MISS RICHARDS. Good night.

FRANCIS. And good night to you.

(MISS RICHARDS *goes out* U. R. *with* HARRIS.)

DOUGLAS. The Bollinger '33.

FRANCIS. We must attend to that. (*Re-enter* HARRIS U. R.) Oh, Harris. If we are wanted, Mr. Douglas and I are down below. (*Exit* FRANCIS U. L. C. *to the cellar.*)

HARRIS. In the cellars, sir, or the dungeons?

DOUGLAS. In the old cellar, Harris.

HARRIS. Very good, sir.

(DOUGLAS *follows* FRANCIS U. L. C. *into the cellar.* HARRIS *looks after them inscrutably, and then turns to go. The door to the hall is opened, and* MISS RICHARDS *hurries on* U. R.)

MISS RICHARDS. I'm so sorry, I left my camera.

HARRIS. (*Picking up camera from chair* R. *of table.*) Here it is, madam.

MISS RICHARDS. I can't afford to lose that. (*Takes camera.*) What a paintbrush is to an artist, this is to me.

HARRIS. Yes, madam. (MISS RICHARDS *turns to go when, from down in the cellars, comes a noise of something being dragged along the ground.*)

MISS RICHARDS. Good gracious me! What's that?

HARRIS. Mr. Francis, and Mr. Douglas.

MISS RICHARDS. What? Where?

HARRIS. Below.

MISS RICHARDS. (*Peering down cellar stairs.*) Down those great, dark, dirty stairs?

HARRIS. They are very hard to keep clean, madam.

MISS RICHARDS. What are they doing there?

HARRIS. I have no idea.

(HARRIS *continues his task of clearing the table, quite unperturbed.* MISS RICHARDS *is intrigued by the noise. There is another noise, louder this time.*)

MISS RICHARDS. It sounds like something moving, don't you think?

HARRIS. Very likely, madam.

MISS RICHARDS. What have you got down there?

HARRIS. Dungeons, cellars, torture chamber . . .

MISS RICHARDS. Torture chamber!

HARRIS. It is not still in use as such, madam, at least, not regularly.

MISS RICHARDS. But it's still there?

HARRIS. Yes, indeed. Parts are bricked up. But the dungeons can still be opened by locks, and bolts, and chains.

MISS RICHARDS. Dungeons! Whatever could they want them for to-day?

HARRIS. Tax-collectors, billeting officers, ladies selling raffle tickets, and the like. Last year a Sunday school picnic got locked down there for the day.

MISS RICHARDS. How awful!

HARRIS. It did them the world of good, madam. They came out singing hymns as they had never sung before.

MISS RICHARDS. You sound as though you liked living near such frightening things.

HARRIS. I admire the past, madam, and things which resist change.

MISS RICHARDS. You are going to be a little upset, I suppose, by the present arrangement.

HARRIS. You are referring to my change of masters?

MISS RICHARDS. Miss Oberon arrives to-night. (*About to make notes.*)

HARRIS. I should not dream of discussing the family, madam.

MISS RICHARDS. Of course not. (*Puts notes away.*)

HARRIS. I shall serve Miss Oberon with the devotion I served her great-grandmother.

MISS RICHARDS. You have been here as long as that?

HARRIS. I came as a youth from the village, madam, when the world was very different. In those days it was an honour for me. I have remained as a servant ever since. Others have come and gone. Some were ambitious. Some went when the family were too impoverished to pay.

MISS RICHARDS. Why did you stay?

HARRIS. I have my place here. I am part of it.

FRANCIS. (*Speaking from the shadow at the top of the cellar stairs.*) Are you talking again, Harris?

HARRIS. I'm afraid so, sir.

MISS RICHARDS. I beg your pardon. It was all my fault. I forgot my camera, and Harris proved entrancing.

FRANCIS. It is a habit of his. I hope you haven't been annoyed.

MISS RICHARDS. Indeed no. Most interested. Now I must go, and take no more of your time. Good-bye.

(HARRIS *goes out with her* U. R. DOUGLAS *comes up the steps, brushing dust off his trousers.*)

DOUGLAS. The bait is precariously poised in the snare. Now we must coax the vixen to put her nose in the trap, and a paw on the spring.

FRANCIS. That woman was here again.

DOUGLAS. What woman?

FRANCIS. The journalist.

DOUGLAS. What for?

FRANCIS. She said she'd left her camera. Harris was talking to her.

DOUGLAS. How long was she here?

FRANCIS. I don't know.

DOUGLAS. Is she a danger? (*Moving below table.*)

FRANCIS. Possibly.

DOUGLAS. What did she get out of him?

FRANCIS. Nothing, I'll guarantee. (HARRIS *comes in* U. R.) Did you finish the debate on the doorstep, Harris?

HARRIS. No, sir. You recalled me to a proper sense of behaviour.

DOUGLAS. How much did you tell her?

HARRIS. I sketched the ethics of my occupation, sir.

DOUGLAS. Damn your ethics, Harris. What did you tell her about us; about the family: about our cousin coming here?

HARRIS. The lady is a journalist, sir. Credit me please with some propriety. There is a motor-car coming down the drive. (*Exit* HARRIS U. R. *A car can be heard. Lights go past the window.*)

FRANCIS. It must be her.

DOUGLAS. Cousin Toni.

FRANCIS. That woman put her clean out of my head.

DOUGLAS. We look perfectly all right? No cobwebs on our clothes? No dust on our hands?

FRANCIS. Is everything in order?

DOUGLAS. Everything is in place.

FRANCIS. You had better stand on that side. I'll stand on this.

DOUGLAS. We'll rise to meet her.

(*The great DOOR-BELL rings. They dress the stage with apparent nonchalance, one on one side, one on the other. After a moment, HARRIS re-enters U. R. and stands to one side. TONI comes in. She is beautifully dressed in soft furs. Her head is a mass of curls; her face, round, lovely, innocent. Her eyes wander round the great room. Her lips are an "oh." She is young, lovely, lost, and most adorable. The two men rise slowly. They are still perfectly under control, but half a second slower in their reactions as she is so unexpectedly beautiful. FRANCIS is the first to smile. A light creeps over his face. He speaks softly as he goes towards her.*)

HARRIS. Miss Oberon.

FRANCIS. Cousin Toni. (*She looks at him with big, frightened eyes as FRANCIS comes behind her and takes off her fur cape. DOUGLAS is almost purring. He is rubbing his hands together gently as he looks at her.*)

DOUGLAS. You have no idea how pleased we are to see you, cousin Toni.

SLOW CURTAIN

ACT I

SCENE 2

The same: the following morning. The sofa has been brought down to R. of centre-stage. The table is up-stage against wall in angle of stairs in place of sofa. The chairs are against wall. HARRIS, with a green apron round him, is polishing silver and swords at the table. The front DOOR-BELL rings. He puts down the sword he is breathing on, and goes out U. R. As he walks back on again he is conducting MISS RICHARDS.

HARRIS. Yes, madam. She arrived last night.

MISS RICHARDS. (D. R. *to sofa.*) Did she get my message?

HARRIS. (*Above sofa.*) Mr. Douglas told her you would call at noon.

MISS RICHARDS. I'm a little early. May I wait?

HARRIS. Of course, madam.

MISS RICHARDS. (*Sits.*) How does Miss Oberon feel this morning, after her travels?

HARRIS. I do not know, madam. I have not seen her to-day.

MISS RICHARDS. Indeed?

HARRIS. I fancy she is still asleep.

MISS RICHARDS. At twelve o'clock!

HARRIS. A quarter to.

MISS RICHARDS. Is it not rather late?

HARRIS. Miss Oberon must be tired after her journey.

MISS RICHARDS. Which room is she sleeping in?

HARRIS. She has the guest-room at present.

MISS RICHARDS. Good gracious me! I thought something terrible once happened there.

HARRIS. Not once, madam. Several times. Miss Oberon was fully warned about its gruesome history.

MISS RICHARDS. Then why has she gone there?

HARRIS. Apparently she does not believe in sliding panels, and figures behind doors.

MISS RICHARDS. What!

HARRIS. Miss Oberon is not superstitious.

MISS RICHARDS. But her cousins. Where are they? Surely they must be growing a little apprehensive.

HARRIS. I doubt it, madam. Mr. Francis and Mr. Douglas seldom rise before noon. Did you wish to see either of them?

MISS RICHARDS. No, but . . .

HARRIS. Ah! How very fortunate. Here they are.

(FRANCIS *and* DOUGLAS *are coming down the staircase. They put on their morning smile as they see* MISS RICHARDS. HARRIS *begins to polish swords again.*)

FRANCIS. (*To* R. *of sofa.*) Good morning, Miss Richards. How good of you to be so prompt.

DOUGLAS. Cousin Toni said she would be glad to see you precisely as the hour struck.

MISS RICHARDS. But I have heard the lady is still asleep.

FRANCIS. (*Moving to fireplace.*) Indeed?

HARRIS. (*At table.*) I passed by her door some few moments ago, sir. There was no sound of movement from within.

DOUGLAS. (*Above sofa.*) She promised she would not be late. She prides herself on punctuality.

MISS RICHARDS. I was a little anxious when I heard that she was in *that* room.

·FRANCIS. Wasn't that a coincidence? Here we were discussing that dreadful room with you, and on her first night she insists on sleeping there.

MISS RICHARDS. Couldn't you have stopped her?

DOUGLAS. We were entirely against it. Weren't we, Harris?

HARRIS. So it appeared, sir.

DOUGLAS. But we are no longer masters. Miss Oberon may do what she likes and go where she pleases.

MISS RICHARDS. Yes, I suppose so.

FRANCIS. Stroll past the guest-room door, Harris.

HARRIS. Very good, sir. (*Moves to bottom of stairs.*)

FRANCIS. Listen for breathing.

HARRIS. Yes, sir.

(HARRIS *turns to climb stairs.* DOUGLAS *calls after him.*)

DOUGLAS. Oh, by the way, Harris. You didn't hear a scream in the night?

HARRIS. Yes, sir. I did.

MISS RICHARDS. Miss Oberon!

HARRIS. No, madam. It was I. I stubbed my toe on the mahogany upright as I leaped into my bed. (*Exit* HARRIS *upstairs.*)

FRANCIS. (*Making conversation briskly.*) And how long do you intend to stay, Miss Richards?

MISS RICHARDS. Only until I have written my article. Oh, and I should like to take some photographs of the house.

FRANCIS. I am sure Miss Oberon will be delighted to show you round. Why don't you stay a little, after we have gone?

MISS RICHARDS. Do you leave so soon?

DOUGLAS. At the earliest possible moment.

FRANCIS. We do not wish to embarrass Miss Oberon.

MISS RICHARDS. Have you no regrets?

DOUGLAS. None whatever!

FRANCIS. I think you will be able to testify how gaily we resigned our rights.

MISS RICHARDS. I can indeed. (HARRIS *enters from the stairs.*)

FRANCIS. Yes, Harris?

HARRIS. I passed by Miss Oberon's door, sir. I stopped . . .

FRANCIS. Don't dramatise the situation, Harris. What did you hear?

HARRIS. Nothing, sir.

DOUGLAS. Harris, you're as deaf as a post!

HARRIS. Yes, sir.

DOUGLAS. Don't give it a thought, Miss Richards. On one occasion he did not even hear Aunt Agricola trapped in the pantry a day and a half.

HARRIS. Madam, if you saw our pantry . . .

FRANCIS. Don't protest, Harris. Make yourself useful. Miss Richards wishes to take some photographs. Please conduct her to the baronial hall. Show her the Crusader's Grave under the table, and the view from the Devil's Jump.

HARRIS. This way, madam.

(*Exit* HARRIS D. L., *showing* MISS RICHARDS *off, along passage which leads to rest of house. This passage opening need have no visible door.*)

FRANCIS. (*Moving in to* DOUGLAS.) What a wonderful piece of luck, Douglas. As long as that woman is in the house, we will have a watertight alibi. This is the moment. Something must happen to Toni, here and now . . . practically in her presence.

DOUGLAS. Francis, you have a fine capacity for seeing things clearly and logically.

FRANCIS. You think so, Douglas? Thank you. (HARRIS *enters from passage* D. L.) You have left Miss Richards in the hall?

HARRIS. Yes, sir.

FRANCIS. Good.

DOUGLAS. Harris, knock at Miss Oberon's door and see if she has overslept.

HARRIS. Yes, sir. (*Exit* HARRIS *upstairs.*)

DOUGLAS. Nothing must happen to Toni while she is

with us alone; that is the only danger. When something unfortunate accounts for her, our alibi must be at hand.

FRANCIS. Douglas, there is a masterly touch about your machinations.

DOUGLAS. You think so, Francis? Thank you. (*Enter* MISS RICHARDS *from* D. L.)

MISS RICHARDS. Thank you, gentlemen. I have taken a lovely photograph. Do you think Miss Oberon . . . (HARRIS *comes hurrying down the stairs.*)

HARRIS. Mr. Francis! Mr. Douglas!

DOUGLAS. What is it, Harris?

FRANCIS. What is the meaning of this uproar?

HARRIS. Miss Oberon, sir! Miss Oberon has gone!

FRANCIS. Gone, Harris? What do you mean? Gone?

DOUGLAS. How could she be gone? Talk sense, Harris.

HARRIS. I have been into her room, sir. Miss Oberon is nowhere to be seen.

MISS RICHARDS. Were her clothes there?

HARRIS. I never thought to look, madam.

DOUGLAS. But she can't have gone. Nothing can have happened yet.

MISS RICHARDS. Then, where is she?

DOUGLAS. Don't worry. We'll soon find out. (DOUGLAS *goes to the foot of the stairs. Shouting.*) Toni! Cousin Toni!

MISS RICHARDS. Well?

DOUGLAS. (*Barking his directions like a captain in the field.*) Look in the gallery, Francis: in the kitchen, Harris. (FRANCIS *disappears like a shot up stairs.* HARRIS *hurries* D. L. DOUGLAS *goes out* U. R. *into the hall.* DOUGLAS *is back almost at once.*) Not there. (FRANCIS *reenters from stairs.*)

FRANCIS. She isn't up there.

MISS RICHARDS. I suppose, in a house like this, she might be anywhere.

DOUGLAS. Anywhere, Miss Richards, absolutely anywhere. (*Enter* HARRIS *from* D. L.)

HARRIS. She isn't there, sir!

DOUGLAS. But she must be found.

FRANCIS. If she's done something silly, or gone anywhere dangerous: Douglas! I hope in heaven's name she hasn't gone down there.

DOUGLAS. The cellars!

MISS RICHARDS. The torture chamber! Oh, quickly, quickly. We must look.

DOUGLAS. Perhaps you're right, Miss Richards. We ought to look. We all ought to look. (*The brothers are on either side; as they move towards the cellar, she is edged along with them.*)

MISS RICHARDS. Oh! You really need me?

DOUGLAS. We shall want every help.

MISS RICHARDS. Very well.

(*As DOUGLAS and FRANCIS move to the opening of the cellar steps, with MISS RICHARDS between them, there is heard coming from outside, the sound of a girl singing. All freeze at the top of the steps. The clock is striking twelve. With complete composure HARRIS announces.*)

HARRIS. Miss Oberon.

(*Fresh and gay as the spring day, TONI walks in from the front door U. R. The cousins come down on either side to greet her. HARRIS goes out U. R.*)

FRANCIS. Good morning, Cousin Toni.

DOUGLAS. We trust you slept well?

TONI. I slept beautifully. I hope you didn't mind my getting up. I woke about six o'clock. The sun was shining and the park looked exquisite. I could not resist it. I have wandered in and out of formal garden, orchard, parkland. I have climbed the Jacobean Tower, and explored the hollow caves. I have visited the disused quarry, and gone along the old cliff face. In fact, I don't think there is a dangerous, difficult, tricky, treacherous part of the estate which I haven't seen. It's been wonderful; like a challenge. I've had a most exciting, delightful, magnificent morning.

DOUGLAS. You've been along the old cliff face?

TONI. Yes. Wicked, isn't it. It looks so safe on the surface, but oh, how it crumbles underfoot! That's not a place for a dark night, is it? (*Moving a step to* DOUGLAS.)

DOUGLAS. No.

FRANCIS. And the Jacobean Tower? Did you say you'd climbed the Jacobean Tower?

TONI. Right to the top. To the slippery edge, where a gust of wind might blow you sixty feet down to the iron railings. And that's not a place for a windy day, is it?

FRANCIS. No.

DOUGLAS. And the caves, cousin Toni. Have you been down the underground caverns?

TONI. I have.

FRANCIS. And the disused quarry?

TONI. I saw that, too.

DOUGLAS. You haven't left us much to show you, cousin Toni.

TONI. (*Turning away from them both to fireplace.*) You will find other things I am sure. (MISS RICHARDS *gives a little cough.*)

FRANCIS. Oh, do forgive us. This is Miss Richards. You remember? She said she would be here at twelve o'clock.

(FRANCIS *steps back to present* MISS RICHARDS *to* TONI. MISS RICHARDS *crosses to* TONI.)

TONI. Of course I remember. That was why I came back. Otherwise I would still be exploring this enchanted estate.

MISS RICHARDS. It was very good of you to let me call.

TONI. Not at all. We are honoured. I thought that perhaps this morning you might like to take your photographs.

MISS RICHARDS. Exactly what I want to do.

TONI. Then later we could have our chat.

MISS RICHARDS. Perfect. I've already taken the hall. I'd love to do the gallery.

TONI. Francis, will that be all right?

FRANCIS. Dear Toni, the house is yours. You do not need our permission.

TONI. I thought there might be certain rooms—

DOUGLAS. Miss Richards is very welcome to photograph the entire house. We have nothing to hide.

TONI. In that case, Miss Richards, please come with me. I'll show you the Oak Gallery.

(*Exeunt* TONI *with* MISS RICHARDS, *up the stairs. The two men look after them, turning back on audience, and watching* TONI *out of sight.*)

DOUGLAS. Well, what do you think? (*Both men are* U. C.)

FRANCIS. The sooner we get this over and done with the better: otherwise cousin Toni will have explored the whole estate.

DOUGLAS. She's already ruled out four complete certainties.

FRANCIS. Beginner's luck.

DOUGLAS. But the tower, the caves, the quarry, *and* the cliffs?

FRANCIS. My dear Douglas, with the loose supports in the cellar below, we shall require none of these accessories.

DOUGLAS. Be quiet, she's coming back. (*Breaks away towards fireplace. Enter* TONI *from stairs, speaking as she goes* C. *between them.*)

TONI. I'm so sorry you should be disturbed like this, my first morning here. I hadn't expected her so soon.

FRANCIS. (D. L.) We are only too pleased to have the old house in the news.

TONI. It's only a stuffy ladies' magazine.

FRANCIS. What could be more delightful?

TONI. (C.) I left her in the gallery. She says there's enough to keep her busy all day.

DOUGLAS. She isn't going to stay all day? (*Moves in to* TONI.)

TONI. Of course not. I'll ask her to go now, if you don't like her there.

FRANCIS. (*Moving in to* TONI.) No, no, Toni. We are delighted to have Miss Richards here this morning. Douglas was only joking. You will get used to his sense of humour in time. (*Both men close in to her.*)

TONI. I am sure I shall. I shall get used to it in no time. I have been here only a few hours and yet everything seems so familiar. I know each nook and cranny. I might have been here all my life.

DOUGLAS. You do seem to have found your way around very quickly.

TONI. It was second nature. It's as if I had been here before. (*Moves away* D. S. *from them, looking up thoughtfully, a little fey.*)

FRANCIS. (*Anxiously watching her.*) You haven't, have you?

TONI. (*Moving* D. L., *then swinging innocently up to cellar opening.*) Only in dreams: often I have dreamed about this house; but, even in my dreams, it was never so lovely.

FRANCIS. We are glad you are pleased.

TONI. (*To* FRANCIS.) But I'm not pleased, I'm dejected. This place is yours. It's really yours. It lives and breathes like *you*.

DOUGLAS. That is hardly surprising.

TONI. And yet it also feels like mine.

FRANCIS. It is yours, cousin Toni.

TONI. And now you are forced to share it with a stranger.

FRANCIS. You are no stranger.

TONI. If only I could give it back to you.

DOUGLAS. (*Crossing to sofa.*) That is impossible. The whole estate is rigidly entailed. Since great-grandmamma has died we have been wrong in staying here.

TONI. Oh, no, you shall stay. No one can turn you

out. As long as it is mine, you shall remain. It will be your home.

FRANCIS. You are very kind but . . .

TONI. I need someone to manage the estate. You must stay. You must help.

FRANCIS. We were totally unprepared for this, Cousin.

TONI. 'Please!

FRANCIS. Very well. Since you are so kind.

TONI. Oh, I am glad. (*Turning to* DOUGLAS.) And you, Douglas?

DOUGLAS. Francis speaks for us both.

TONI. Now, I really am happy. I won't alter a stone of it without your consent. You must tell me all that is required. It is so like a human being, this old house.

DOUGLAS. And, like a human being, it has its darker side.

TONI. I don't believe it.

FRANCIS. I assure you. Not only do you have its handsome façade, its solid frame and massive walls, its arches and its timbering; but you have its shadowy foundations: the unseen origins on which it stands, like the subconscious of the human mind.

DOUGLAS. You have its grim, dark passages below.

TONI. I can believe nothing evil of this house. I feel so safe in it, so well protected. I would not be afraid in its dark passages.

DOUGLAS. Perhaps you would change your mind if you went into the cellars.

TONI. That shows you don't know me very well yet. Down there? Why, I'd go at once if I didn't have Miss Richards on my hands. (*Crossing below sofa and* U. S. *to stairs.*)

DOUGLAS. We could always look after her.

TONI. No . . . I really must see if she is all right. But afterwards! Oh, Francis, Douglas: won't it be exciting!

(*Exit* TONI, *up stairs.* FRANCIS *looks after her thoughtfully, hesitates, then decides to sound* DOUGLAS.)

FRANCIS. It seems a pity, doesn't it.

DOUGLAS. What does?

FRANCIS. She's so obviously out to please; so pathetically anxious to be fair to us; so ready to pour money into our estate.

DOUGLAS. It's money she can well afford.

FRANCIS. Such an innocent nature: sweet, gentle, affectionate; so trusting.

DOUGLAS. All the easier for us.

FRANCIS. It's a shame there is no other way. (*Sits on table edge.*)

DOUGLAS. What are you suggesting? (*Sits on sofa.*)

FRANCIS. Sadly reflecting that we have rejected marriage.

DOUGLAS. We could, of course, give it reconsideration.

FRANCIS. I'm glad you think so.

DOUGLAS. If you do not think it foolish to alter tack once we have set our course?

FRANCIS. I think it advisable. Marriage could be an excellent solution. She is so childish and unworldly, like putty in our hands. She would be no difficulty at all. Do let us reconsider marriage.

DOUGLAS. It might surprise you to learn I have already done so.

FRANCIS. Indeed?

DOUGLAS. Last night I gave the subject a good deal of thought.

FRANCIS. Last night?

DOUGLAS. Yes. After I saw the girl.

FRANCIS. How can that make any difference? I was prepared to marry her before. I still am.

DOUGLAS. I meant, Francis, to marry her myself.

FRANCIS. (*Gets up—alarmed.*) My dear Douglas. What are you saying? Marriage was my suggestion. I attend to that.

DOUGLAS. But last night you refused to consider such a solution.

FRANCIS. Nonsense, Douglas. I advocated marriage.

DOUGLAS. Yes . . . for me.

FRANCIS. And you turned it down.

DOUGLAS. I was grossly ill-informed.

FRANCIS. So was I. Anyhow, all the essentials were correct. (*Moving in towards* DOUGLAS.)

DOUGLAS. What! Flat! Plain! . . .

FRANCIS. These are not essentials.

DOUGLAS. Francis! If I have to live the rest of my life with Toni . . .

FRANCIS. But it is not you, it is I.

DOUGLAS. I marry the girl, or no one.

FRANCIS. Why are you so unreasonable?

DOUGLAS. If you insist on killing the girl . . .

FRANCIS. But it is you . . .

DOUGLAS. My dear Francis! Let us not continue the debate at this vital moment. The bait lies poised on a hairspring; four tons of debris suspended over the victim's head; our cousin panting to try her luck; our alibi waiting to swear our innocence? This is no time for differences.

FRANCIS. Of course not, Douglas. What is our next step?

DOUGLAS. When she returns, I shall suggest a drink to celebrate her visit. I will seize the opportunity to show her the way below. The rest is easy. (*Enter* HARRIS *from* U. R.)

FRANCIS. Oh, Harris, we intend using the old cellars again. (*Moving* D. L. *to sideboard.*)

HARRIS. Is that not dangerous, sir?

DOUGLAS. Why should it be?

HARRIS. (*Moving* D. C.) It's been unsafe for some time, sir.

DOUGLAS. Nonsense. We've never had an accident. Not a fatal one.

HARRIS. No, sir.

DOUGLAS. Then don't argue, Harris. The Bollinger '33 is now in the old cellar.

HARRIS. Very good, sir. (*He goes out* D. L.)

DOUGLAS. It's just as well to establish the situation beforehand.

(*Enter* TONI *and* MISS RICHARDS *from the stairs.*)

MISS RICHARDS. Thank you so much, gentlemen. It's been most good of you. I've taken some delightful photos of the gallery.

FRANCIS. We are glad. Won't you have a drink before you go? I was about to ring for Harris. I thought we might get a bottle from below.

TONI. What a sweet idea!

DOUGLAS. You shouldn't send for Harris. This is Toni's opportunity.

FRANCIS. What do you mean?

DOUGLAS. This is her chance to see the terrors of the deep.

TONI. Of course, I'd love to go. (*Crossing to top of cellar steps.*)

FRANCIS. No, we can't have you doing that.

DOUGLAS. She said she wouldn't be afraid.

TONI. I'm not.

(DOUGLAS *and* FRANCIS *have moved in on either side of her.*)

FRANCIS. If you insist. It's the sharp turning to the left as you reach the bottom of the steps. Bend low or you'll hit the roof.

MISS RICHARDS. (D. R.) Miss Oberon! You aren't going down there?

TONI. Why not?

DOUGLAS. Why not, indeed! There's nothing in the dungeons now, you know.

MISS RICHARDS. It looks so dark. You don't even know the way.

DOUGLAS. I'm going with her. She'll be quite safe.

TONI. No, I'll go myself.

FRANCIS. You must let Douglas go with you.

TONI. I insist. I go by myself or not at all.

FRANCIS. Very well.

TONI. Sharp left, and bend my head. (*She goes down-stairs into the cellar.* MISS RICHARDS *sits on sofa. She is disapproving.*)

FRANCIS. Did you notice how keen she was to go, Miss Richards? She's been talking about those cellars ever since she arrived.

MISS RICHARDS. You shouldn't have let her go.

DOUGLAS. How could we stop her?

FRANCIS. Miss Oberon is of age, and capable of looking after herself.

MISS RICHARDS. She may get lost. She may stumble and fall. She might hurt herself.

DOUGLAS. (*Crossing above sofa.*) Most unlikely. (*There is a long pause. They listen.*)

FRANCIS. (*Crossing to top of cellar steps.*) I don't hear a thing.

DOUGLAS. Neither do I. Not a sound. What the devil's happened?

FRANCIS. Listen!

DOUGLAS. Something's gone wrong. I'm going down to make certain. (*He goes downstairs into the cellar.*)

MISS RICHARDS. Where is he going?

FRANCIS. To help Miss Oberon. Perhaps you were right. It was silly of us to let her go down by herself.

(*There is a loud noise of falling masonry.*)

MISS RICHARDS. (*Jumping up.*) What's that!

FRANCIS. Good gracious. Something seems to have collapsed. Let us hope cousin Toni was well clear of it.

MISS RICHARDS. Good heavens! Part of the roof must have fallen in.

FRANCIS. What a dreadful thing!

TONI. (*Off.*) Help! Help!

MISS RICHARDS. (*Hurrying to cellar opening.*) That's her. She's been hurt. She's been trapped. We must go down and help.

FRANCIS. (*Restraining her.*) Douglas will attend to her.

(*There is another FALL, and* TONI *gives a scream. Then there is silence.*)

MISS RICHARDS. (*Horrified.*) What's happened?

FRANCIS. Perhaps I ought to go and see. (*He goes to the top of the steps. He is about to descend when he stops, looks down and recoils with horror.* TONI'S *voice is heard calling.*)

TONI. Francis, Francis. Help me!

MISS RICHARDS. What is it? (*She hurries to join* FRANCIS.) Miss Oberon!

(TONI *staggers up the stairs into the room. She is dragging the stunned body of* DOUGLAS.)

TONI. Help me, Francis. Something seems to have fallen on cousin Douglas. (*The body falls heavily to the floor.*)

CURTAIN

ACT II

Scene 1

The same: a few days later; evening.

As the curtain rises, FRANCIS *is sitting alone on the sofa, reading. He glances up as* HARRIS *wheels in* DOUGLAS *in an invalid chair through archway,* D. L.

DOUGLAS. Don't bang me about, damn you, Harris.

HARRIS. I'm very sorry, sir.

FRANCIS. How are you, Douglas?

DOUGLAS. I'd be a lot better if Harris would give my broken bones a chance.

HARRIS. I did my best, sir.

DOUGLAS. He took me over every bump, every stone, every pitch and toss on the whole estate. It's obvious he doesn't want me to walk again.

FRANCIS. What was the doctor's verdict?

DOUGLAS. He said it would be at least three weeks before I can even stand up. But what with Harris wheeling me around like a ship in a storm it will be more like three years.

HARRIS. He had one slight mishap, sir—on the grass verge. Nothing more.

FRANCIS. Mr. Douglas is not his usual, judicial self while an invalid.

HARRIS. I understand, sir.

FRANCIS. His leg is giving him a great deal of pain.

DOUGLAS. And he kept me out in the damp, evening air.

HARRIS. The doctor said fresh air, sir.

FRANCIS. That will do, Harris. I understand. (HARRIS *bows and goes out* D. L.)

DOUGLAS. Clumsy devil.

(DOUGLAS *can sit in the chair and spin the wheels, which he does, moving over to the fireplace and turning chair to face* FRANCIS.)

FRANCIS. I'll push you around myself in future.

DOUGLAS. To be quite frank, you are not much better.

FRANCIS. Perhaps cousin Toni . . .

DOUGLAS. She at least showed a little care and attention for me. She took me down the road this morning, and only pitched me on my nose once.

FRANCIS. I noticed she had been very solicitous. That should make things much easier.

DOUGLAS. I had thought of that. Nothing like being at the mercy of a woman's loving care for winning her confidence. We are as thick as thieves now, Toni and I.

FRANCIS. Most satisfactory. And when is the endeavour?

DOUGLAS. To-night.

FRANCIS. But my dear Douglas, how can it be?

DOUGLAS. Harris is driving you down to the station?

FRANCIS. Yes.

DOUGLAS. Then she and I will be alone.

FRANCIS. That's true. But what can you do in this condition?

DOUGLAS. Exactly! What can I do, a cripple, a man confined to his wheel-chair, in pain, in agony, unable to stand on his feet for weeks? How could such a man ever walk? When cousin Toni is found strangled in her room upstairs, what suspicion could anyone attach to me?

FRANCIS. (*Still sitting, turns to look closely at* DOUGLAS.) You are distracted, Douglas. I think this accident has jarred you mentally.

DOUGLAS. I have been jarred indeed, Francis. Jarred in every way but mentally. Look.

(FRANCIS *watches, fascinated, as* DOUGLAS *rises slowly, painfully, from his chair and walks a step or two.*)

FRANCIS. You can walk! (*He is astounded.*)

DOUGLAS. Each step I take nearly kills me. But I can walk.

FRANCIS. The doctor—

DOUGLAS. Yes, I know. It's enough to keep most men in their beds a month. And I let him think it was worse than it is. It's alibis we need now, Francis, and this leg of mine is one we want. (*He is back in his chair.*)

FRANCIS. (*Getting up and going to* DOUGLAS.) My dear Douglas! What a heaven-sent blessing! What are you going to do?

DOUGLAS. I will catch her when she is off her guard down here. Then I will carry the body to her room. I will 'phone the police, and tell them I have heard sounds of a struggle upstairs, but am unable to investigate in my wheel chair.

FRANCIS. (*Beside* DOUGLAS *at fireplace.*) I believe you have hit on the very plan.

DOUGLAS. Trust me. I'm not likely to give up because of a set-back at the first endeavour.

FRANCIS. (*Turning away thoughtfully, and going slowly to sofa.*) That was extraordinary, wasn't it, that affair in the cellar?

DOUGLAS. It was devilish bad luck, and devilish heavy bricks. Another step and it would have been all up with me.

FRANCIS. (*Above sofa.*) I can't make it out. Where was she? How did Toni get out of the way?

DOUGLAS. I was too occupied in keeping the roof off my head to notice.

FRANCIS. I can't understand it.

DOUGLAS. Forget it. No good will come of contemplating our failures. This time we will succeed.

FRANCIS. I was wondering if she could possibly suspect.

DOUGLAS. What could she suspect?

FRANCIS. (*Moving* U. L.) I don't know. But it seems funny that she should have got out of there alive.

DOUGLAS. It was the merest chance, I tell you, a piece

of luck, an accident. If she had not seen a big, black rat and run the other way—

FRANCIS. (*Prowling back to* C.) That's her story.

DOUGLAS. You know the cellars are full of rats.

FRANCIS. (U. R.) I think it was a most opportune rat for anyone to have encountered.

DOUGLAS. Don't be so exasperating. What on earth could she know? What could she guess? That we were trying to bury her under a fallen wall? If she guessed that, why did she go?

FRANCIS. She may have suspected us since.

DOUGLAS. If she guesses we tried to kill her, then she might know we would try it again.

FRANCIS. (*Quickly goes to* DOUGLAS *at fireplace.*) Yes, that's what I mean.

DOUGLAS. (*Triumphantly.*) Then, in that case, why does she stay?

FRANCIS. (*Stumped.*) I don't know.

DOUGLAS. Don't be silly, Francis. It isn't logical.

FRANCIS. (*Moving* U. R. *of sofa.*) I suppose not.

DOUGLAS. Besides, does she act as if she feared any harm? Not a bit of it. She's as meek and mild, as sweet and friendly, as ever I hope to see anyone. I'd like to wager that she will let me put this scarf around her neck to-night, to let me see it match the colour of her hair.

FRANCIS. (*To fireplace* D. R.) I hope you're right.

DOUGLAS. Of course I am.

FRANCIS. Good luck, in any case. You will not have much time. Harris is driving me down to the station. I shall make some inquiries and come back.

DOUGLAS. How long will that be?

FRANCIS. Fifteen minutes.

DOUGLAS. Time enough to make sure of a dozen fortunes. Leave it to me. (HARRIS *enters* D. L.)

HARRIS. I was about to bring the car round, sir. (*Moving towards front door.*)

FRANCIS. Very good, Harris.

HARRIS. (C.) Is Miss Oberon coming with us, sir?

FRANCIS. Why should she, Harris?

HARRIS. I merely wondered whether to take one rug or two.

FRANCIS. No, Harris. Miss Oberon is not coming.

HARRIS. Very good, sir. (*Making for front door.*)

DOUGLAS. Miss Oberon has said she is happy to stay and look after me.

HARRIS. How very kind, sir. (*Exit U. R.*)

FRANCIS. What do you suppose Harris thinks?

DOUGLAS. What Harris thinks he will keep to himself. He belongs to the house.

FRANCIS. But which side of the house might he choose to support?

DOUGLAS. When she's dispatched he will accept the *fait accompli.* That's the only reality. He needs nothing more.

FRANCIS. Neither do we. (*Enter* TONI *from stairs.*)

TONI. And how is the poor invalid this evening?

DOUGLAS. Not too bright, thank you, Toni.

TONI. What a shame!

FRANCIS. And he's a little sharp-tempered, too, so you'll have to excuse him.

TONI. I quite understand. I think he's a fine, brave boy not to make more fuss. I know if it had been me, I'd have given up the ghost by now.

FRANCIS. Even Douglas can say he is glad it happened to him, not you.

DOUGLAS. Anything, rather than that.

TONI. How sweet of you. (TONI *picks up the scarf which has fallen beside* DOUGLAS's *chair, and puts it round his neck.* DOUGLAS *sits very still.*) Take care of yourself, Douglas. You mustn't catch cold. (*Stepping away to* C.) I looked everywhere this afternoon in the village for something nice for you. The shops were shutting, but I managed to get you a pineapple and some grapes.

DOUGLAS. A pineapple!

TONI. I asked Harris what was your favourite fruit.

DOUGLAS. That was very considerate. I didn't expect that. Even my brother hasn't bought me a pineapple.

TONI. I met the doctor on my way back. I was most upset. I suppose he told you everything?

DOUGLAS. He kept nothing back.

TONI. Dreadful, isn't it?

FRANCIS. It's not as bad as that. (*Airily, still* D. R., *slightly above* DOUGLAS's *chair.*)

TONI. Francis! Really! How can you say that! How would you like never to be able to stand straight again?

DOUGLAS. What's that?

TONI. He told you that, didn't he?

DOUGLAS. What? Tell me what he said?

TONI. He said—you might never be able to stand again.

DOUGLAS. It's a lie. I can.

TONI. What have I said?

DOUGLAS. Look! I can! I can stand. (*He is struggling to his feet.*)

FRANCIS. Douglas! What do you think you're doing? (*Holding* DOUGLAS *down.*)

DOUGLAS. Help me. I can!

FRANCIS. Keep still, you fool! You cannot stand. You cannot get up. It will be weeks before you walk again. In fact you may never walk. (*Pressing* DOUGLAS *back into his chair.*)

DOUGLAS. Why, yes. Of course. I was forgetting. How foolish. No, of course I cannot stand. Did he say I never would?

TONI. He said something like that. Perhaps I was mistaken. He was in a hurry. I didn't hear him properly.

DOUGLAS. I think that was an exaggeration. But he's right, of course. It will take some time.

TONI. (*Kneeling beside* DOUGLAS's *chair.*) How sorry I am to have upset you so. I thought the doctor told you. I am sure you will get better, Douglas. You'll be walking in no time.

DOUGLAS. Forgive me. The sudden news made me forget myself.

FRANCIS. I'm sure cousin Toni forgives you. (*He speaks confidentially to* TONI *from the other side of her, as she kneels beside* DOUGLAS.) He is very weak, I'm afraid. I'm sorry I have to go out and leave him this evening. I don't like to, when he is in this excitable condition, but I really must.

TONI. Of course. Do not worry about him. I shall look after Douglas. (*Rising, and crossing* U. C. *to table.*)

FRANCIS. You are very kind. I hope you remember to behave yourself, Douglas. You very nearly did a silly thing. (*Gives* DOUGLAS *a reproving slap on the arm.*)

DOUGLAS. I know.

TONI. (*Turning to the two men.*) Don't scold him. It must be so dull having to sit around all day in that chair.

DOUGLAS. I never find it dull.

TONI. Don't you?

DOUGLAS. I always have my thoughts. (*Enter* HARRIS, U. R.)

HARRIS. I was about to bring the car round, sir, when I saw Miss Richards.

FRANCIS. Who?

HARRIS. The lady journalist.

DOUGLAS. What can she want?

FRANCIS. Are you expecting her?

TONI. (*Beside table.*) No. I can't think what she wants. Where is she, Harris?

HARRIS. She is walking along the drive.

DOUGLAS. Push me out of here, will you, Francis. I can't stand news-hawks at the best of times, and I certainly don't want company as long as I'm in this ridiculous chair. (*Wheels himself across stage to exit* D. L.)

TONI. What a nuisance.

FRANCIS. Perhaps cousin Toni will soon get rid of her.

TONI. I'll try.

FRANCIS. We could drive her to the village when we go. (*Hurries after* DOUGLAS *and begins to push chair off.*)

TONI. A good idea: we don't want anything to disturb Douglas, as long as he's like this.

DOUGLAS. Thank you, Toni. I knew you'd understand. (*The BELL rings.*)

FRANCIS. Show her in, Harris. We will be in the library. (*He wheels* DOUGLAS *off,* D. L.)

HARRIS. Are you at home, miss?

TONI. (U. C.) I think so, Harris.

(*Exit* HARRIS U. R. *Re-enter with* MISS RICHARDS *from* U. R.)

HARRIS. Miss Richards. (*Exit upstairs.*)

TONI. (*Going towards her, at sofa.*) Good evening, Miss Richards. How nice of you to call.

MISS RICHARDS. Good evening, Miss Oberon. I just popped in to give you the first draft of my article. I do hope you will have time to read it, before I send it to my editor. (*Handing* TONI *papers from bag.*)

TONI. You have finished it so soon? (*Sitting, and inviting* MISS RICHARDS *to sit on chair* D. R. *of sofa.*)

MISS RICHARDS. I dashed it off in a blaze of inspiration. A perfect scoop! Your cousin's accident was a godsend. (*Pulls in her chair chattily towards* TONI *on sofa.*)

TONI. Douglas will be pleased to hear that. (*Reading.*) "Rescue from the ruins." It sounds exciting. When do you wish it back?

MISS RICHARDS. Press day is Friday. Shall we say Thursday, at about this time?

TONI. Certainly.

MISS RICHARDS. And by then we shall know if your cousin is going to be all right.

TONI. I'm sure he is.

MISS RICHARDS. How is he to-day?

TONI. Just managing to get around in a wheel-chair, poor dear.

MISS RICHARDS. Our readers will be enthralled to hear about his progress week by week. When they see this story I haven't the slightest doubt they will adopt him on the "knitting for invalids" page.

TONI. Douglas might be a little embarrassed by that.

MISS RICHARDS. We won't tell him; and then, when

his woollies and mittens arrive, they will come as a great surprise.

TONI. I haven't the slightest doubt.

MISS RICHARDS. Besides, he deserves a little fussing. He's had a very narrow escape. He nearly lost his life!

TONI. Dear me, Miss Richards! I'm sure you don't kill people as easily as that.

MISS RICHARDS. Why, I've heard of some extraordinary accidents happening in this house. They were telling me in the village last night. It's so dilapidated, it seems.

TONI. That's what makes it so intriguing. You don't know what's going to come down on you next.

MISS RICHARDS. Are you sure we're quite safe in this room?

TONI. I think so.

MISS RICHARDS. I shouldn't like to stay here by myself.

TONI. I'm lucky to have my cousins with me.

MISS RICHARDS. That must be very comforting in such a rambling place. After all, you could get lost, and they must know their way about.

TONI. (*Getting up, looking round room.*) Good gracious. The house doesn't worry me. It's so friendly and safe. Don't forget; the halls are haunted by my ancestors. Do you think they would let any harm befall me?

MISS RICHARDS. When part of the foundations collapse on your cousin, it shows your ancestors are not as reliable as they might be.

TONI. Nevertheless, Miss Richards, I am not frightened of this house; nor of anything in, round, or under it. (*The CLOCK strikes. Crossing D. L.*) Now you must excuse me. I am to look after poor Douglas this evening. He is very weak, and can't be left on his own. He is probably so tired that he will go straight to sleep. Then I shall be able to read your article to-night. (*Walks to the bell-pull, which is used to summon HARRIS, and pulls it.*)

MISS RICHARDS. (*Rising.*) Tell me what alterations it needs.

TONI. (*Crossing towards* MISS RICHARDS.) Oh, Miss Richards! A sudden thought. I wondered if you would care to leave your camera with me?

MISS RICHARDS. My camera? (*Moving in towards* TONI, C.)

TONI. I shall take great care of it. It's just that I might be able to take a snap or two, to illustrate your article.

MISS RICHARDS. An excellent idea. (*Closer to* TONI.)

TONI. I can't promise anything worth printing, but I shall do my best. (*Enter* HARRIS *from stairs.* MISS RICHARDS *crosses to* HARRIS.) Miss Richards is going, Harris. Please put this camera very carefully in my room. And now, good night, Miss Richards. I must hurry to poor Douglas. (*Exit* D. L.)

MISS RICHARDS. (*Handing camera to* HARRIS.) This side up, Harris. (*Helps him to hold the camera properly.*)

HARRIS. Yes, madam.

MISS RICHARDS. This is the flash. (*Indicates it.*)

HARRIS. I trust it is quite safe, madam. It is not detonated, so to speak? (*Going* D. R.)

MISS RICHARDS. (*Crossing to him.*) What do you mean?

HARRIS. (U. R.) It will not explode?

MISS RICHARDS. It is a camera, Harris, not a bomb.

HARRIS. Very good, madam.

(*Enter* FRANCIS *from* D. L. MISS RICHARDS *crosses to him, but he gently propels her back with him towards front door* U. R.)

FRANCIS. Good evening, Miss Richards. My cousin tells me you are returning to the village. Harris is driving me there. Pray, accompany me.

MISS RICHARDS. Thank you so much. (*Exit* HARRIS U. R.)

FRANCIS. And when are you returning to town?

MISS RICHARDS. I must go back in a day or two, now.

FRANCIS. Cousin Toni will be sorry to see you go. I feel my brother and I are but dull company. (*Moving* U. R. *with her towards front door.*)

MISS RICHARDS. She has just told me otherwise.

FRANCIS. I'm glad to hear it. But she will lack feminine society when you are gone.

(TONI *enters* D. L. *wheeling* DOUGLAS *in his chair.*)

TONI. We have come to see you off. Douglas does not like receiving in this chair. It makes him uncomfortable to see a lady stand, while he is unable to.

MISS RICHARDS. (*Speaking from steps leading to front door.*) I think he is lucky, even to be in that chair.

DOUGLAS. If I must be in a chair at all, madam, I am glad it is this. (HARRIS *enters from* U. R.)

HARRIS. (*At front door.*) The car is at the door, sir.

FRANCIS. Very well. This way, Miss Richards. We will not be long, Toni.

TONI. Do not hurry. Douglas is in safe hands. Good night, Miss Richards.

MISS RICHARDS. Good night. (*Turns and goes out*, U. R., *followed by* FRANCIS, *then* HARRIS. *There is the sound of the outer door banging.* DOUGLAS *is in his chair*, C. TONI *is above it.*)

TONI. They've gone. And now we are alone. It always makes me feel cosy to be left in a house after people go out. Does it you?

DOUGLAS. I've never thought about it.

TONI. (*Moving* D. L. *to sideboard for pineapple.*) And now what would you like to do? I've got your pineapple here. Would you like a slice? (*She has it with a knife, on a silver plate.*)

DOUGLAS. That would be delicious.

TONI. You must cut it with glass or silver, you know.

DOUGLAS. What have you there? (*Wheeling his own chair with his hands to* U. R.)

TONI. (*Moving across to him.*) It's glass. Look. (*She*

holds it out to him, standing very close beside him.)
Lovely, isn't it?

DOUGLAS. (*Very fascinated as he looks at the knife, unable to make up his mind.*) Yes, very lovely.

TONI. (*After a slight pause.*) Well? Don't you want a slice?

DOUGLAS. Oh, yes, of course. (*He wakes from his reverie and hands her the knife. She cuts the pineapple and gives him a slice on a silver plate.* DOUGLAS *moves above the fireplace.*) Aren't you having any?

TONI. No, thanks. (*Sits on sofa.*) I've got a book here —an old favourite of mine. I thought it would be nice if I read to you. (*Picks up book.*)

DOUGLAS. There's nothing I'd like better.

TONI. And this is one of the chapters I like most of all. (*Finds her place.* TONI *is sitting on sofa, facing away from* DOUGLAS *to let the light of a little lamp fall on the book. His chair is some steps away, slightly behind. As she reads he slowly undoes the silk scarf about his neck and gently gets to his feet. Then while she is still reading, he takes painful steps towards her, biting his lip with the effort of it. She begins to read.*) "How are you getting on?" said the Cat. "I don't think they play at all fairly," Alice began, "and they all quarrel so badly one can't hear oneself speak." Just then the King asked: "Who are you talking to?" "A Cheshire Cat," said Alice. "Allow me to introduce it." "I don't like the look of it at all," said the King, "it must be removed." "My dear," he called out to the Queen, "I wish you would have this Cat removed." "Off with his head!" she said. (*Looks up and sees* DOUGLAS.) Why, Douglas! (*He is a step or two away.*) You can walk. (*She sits quite still. He smiles reassuringly and then takes another step; she stands up suddenly and holds out her hands.*) How magnificent! Won't Francis be surprised. How brave of you! It takes more than a fall of bricks to kill one of us, doesn't it.

DOUGLAS. (*In pain.*) Give me your hand, Toni. I can't go any further. (*He is near sofa.*)

TONI. Here you are. (*She moves from sofa, turning*

away from him, which takes her a step away from him.)
Come on. Take it. You can do another two steps. Come
on. Come on. (DOUGLAS *takes a step more. She retreats
to* C., *coaxing him kindly.*)

DOUGLAS. I can't. (*Grabs the back of sofa for support
and works round towards her. She backs away.*)

TONI. You are wonderful, Douglas. I'm proud of you.
There's courage! (*Backing* U. C.)

DOUGLAS. Toni. Toni. Help me. Take my arm. Give
me your hand. (*She is moving* U. S.)

TONI. Here I am. (*Moving above sofa.*) Only a couple
of yards. Leave the chair, Douglas. You can stand without it. You can stand on your own two feet. That's the
way. (*He lurches quickly towards her. She steps back a
little, moving* D. L. *He leans on nearest piece of furni-
ture.*)

DOUGLAS. Don't move. Don't go back. Toni. Toni.
What are you doing? You're killing me. (*Drops scarf.*)

TONI. I'm helping you, Douglas. Oh, you've dropped
your scarf. (*She picks it up and holds it out to him.*)
Here. One last effort. One step or two. (D. L.)

DOUGLAS. I can't go any further.

TONI. (D. L.) You can. Don't disappoint me, Douglas.
I'll stand here. I promise you. Over here. (*She puts the
scarf round her neck and stands with hands outstretched
to him.*) Now, come on. Come to me. (*He takes an ago-
nising step or two.*) That's the way. That's better. Come
to Toni. I'm waiting here to help you. I'll look after you,
Douglas. (*His passage is bringing sweat to his face. He
is growing dazed with effort. She does not move. He
manages to totter to her, with outstretched hands. He
just clasps the tips of her fingers, and then he collapses
on the floor.* TONI *hurriedly attends to him.*) You poor
boy. Was it too much for you? Let me help you up.
(*She helps a defeated* DOUGLAS *to his feet. She takes his
arm and half leads him to the sofa.*) And you were doing
so well. You almost managed it. You almost got me.
You've overtaxed yourself: you must rest. (*She is fussing
round him as he lies back on sofa. She sits beside him,*

his scarf round her neck. She is now apparently at his mercy, but in reality she has complete ascendancy over him. Almost instinctively his two hands go out to his scarf; she sits unresisting, looking at him. His hands drop.) You want your scarf?

DOUGLAS. No, thanks. (*He manages to say:*) You keep it, Toni. It goes prettily with the colour of your hair. (*He gives a dry little laugh, as he lies back exhausted. The door opens and* HARRIS *comes in,* U. R.)

HARRIS. Mr. Francis wishes . . . (*He stops as he sees* DOUGLAS *lying back on the couch.* DOUGLAS's *laugh is changing to a cough.*) Good heavens, Miss Oberon, you haven't . . . ?

TONI. Mr. Douglas is not feeling well, Harris. (HARRIS *hurries out* U. R. *calling.*)

HARRIS. Mr. Francis, come quickly. Something terrible has happened! (*He leaves the door open and we can see him in the hall.* FRANCIS *is heard off stage.*)

FRANCIS. (*Off, calmly.*) What is it, Harris? What are you shouting about? What is the matter now? (TONI *moves to fireplace.*)

HARRIS. (*Entering* U. R.) This way, sir. Something tragic. Miss Oberon . . .

FRANCIS. (*As he enters* U. R.) What can have happened to Miss Oberon? (*He stops aghast as he sees the prostrate body of* DOUGLAS.) Good God! Douglas! What has happened to Mr. Douglas? (*He does not see* TONI.)

HARRIS. I don't know, sir. (R., *between* FRANCIS *and* TONI.)

FRANCIS. Go to Miss Oberon's room. See if she is there.

TONI. (*At fireplace.*) Here I am, Francis. (*He spins round to see her as she advances. He might be looking at a ghost.*)

FRANCIS. (D. C.) You!

TONI. Douglas has been trying to do too much. He's overtired, that's all.

FRANCIS. (U. R. *of sofa.*) What has he been trying to do?

Toni. Trying to catch me.

Francis. What!

Toni. You didn't know he could walk, did you? But he can, a little. I tried to help him, and in our excitement he overdid it.

Francis. (*Crosses to above sofa* c.) So this is how you look after him.

Douglas. (*Weakly, from his couch.*) You are wrong, Francis. I am grateful to cousin Toni. I tried to go too far. I should never have got back here if it hadn't been for Toni's help.

Harris. (R. *of* Douglas.) Can I fetch you anything, sir?

Douglas. Not for myself, but bring Miss Oberon a drink. She must have had a trying time.

Toni. I am a little weak. A reaction, I suppose. I think I'll go to bed early to-night. Don't bother with the drink, Harris.

Harris. (*Crossing* u. r.) Very good, miss. (*Exit* d. l.)

Toni. I'm sorry if you think it was my fault, Francis. Perhaps I should not have encouraged him. But I was so proud of him. Good night. (Toni *goes up the stairs. They watch her out of sight, then* Francis *comes quickly across to* Douglas.)

Francis. (*Behind sofa.*) What happened? What's the meaning of this? You look dead. You are wet with perspiration. You've gone as white as a sheet.

Douglas. (*Lying back on sofa.*) I'm finished, old boy.

Francis. You mean you're dying?

Douglas. I'm finished as far as Toni is concerned. I don't know, yet, if she guessed or not. But she had me on the floor a broken man, and only then did she pick me up. Then she put the scarf round her neck and sat as close to me as you please. And I hadn't the guts left in my body to tighten the knot.

Francis. (*Moving* l. c.) You must be mad, or drunk.

Douglas. I'm sober and sane. I know when I've met my match.

FRANCIS. (*Crossing to fireplace.*) Did she know what you intended?

DOUGLAS. It's impossible to say. Not by as much as a look did she show it, if she knew.

FRANCIS. Then we can try again.

DOUGLAS. She's beaten us.

FRANCIS. She has not beaten me. (*Sits in wheel-chair at fireplace.*)

DOUGLAS. Marriage or murder? Would she marry us, now? Not on your life. And I am afraid to fire the shot.

FRANCIS. Very well, I must do it.

DOUGLAS. You! You never could.

FRANCIS. It's to-night or never, I feel. (*Gets up, crosses to* DOUGLAS.) If you are so easily defeated.

DOUGLAS. Easily! My God, man, she nearly broke my heart before I cracked.

FRANCIS. (*Going* U. R.) I bend a lot more than you do, Douglas. Perhaps I don't crack so easily.

DOUGLAS. What do you intend to do?

FRANCIS. I'm going to her room. There isn't a moment to lose. (*Crosses to foot of stairs.*)

DOUGLAS. What have you there?

FRANCIS. It's a glass knife.

DOUGLAS. My pineapple!

FRANCIS. I'm going to turn the lights out.

DOUGLAS. Why? (FRANCIS, *from a switch at foot of stairs, turns out the lights except the one on the landing up the stairs.*)

FRANCIS. Harris must think we have gone to bed. You stay here. I'll push you under the shadow of the alcove. (*Helps* DOUGLAS *into wheel-chair.*)

DOUGLAS. You know I don't like being left alone.

FRANCIS. (*Above sofa,* R.) What has happened to you? You'll be all right. I'll be down in five minutes. (*Pushes chair* U. L. *into shadow.*)

DOUGLAS. As you say.

(FRANCIS *begins to mount the stairs. There is deadly silence. He is slowly going up, holding his knife and looking up at the landing. He stops—then starts again when there is suddenly a voice from behind him, from the shadow of the other side of the landing. It is* TONI.)

TONI. Good night, Francis. (FRANCIS *stiffens with horror. The knife drops from his limp hand.* TONI *comes slowly on.*) I decided I would have that drink after all, so I went down by the servants' staircase. Harris has given me a very strong one. See. (*She holds the glass up. She begins to go up the stairs, passing* FRANCIS, *and then says:*) You've dropped something. Oh, it's the pineapple knife. (*She picks it up and hands it to him.*) Is pineapple your favourite fruit, as well? (*She goes up a step or two more, and then calls back without turning her head.*) Good night, Douglas. (*They are still, deadly still, as she goes out of sight up stairs. Then* FRANCIS *comes stumbling down the steps and switches on all the lights.* DOUGLAS *propels his chair swiftly from the alcove to* U. S. C.)

FRANCIS. Does she know? Does she guess?

DOUGLAS. "Good night, Douglas"?

FRANCIS. Does she know?

DOUGLAS. Well, aren't you going?

FRANCIS. How can I go?

DOUGLAS. (C.) I thought not.

FRANCIS. (*At fireplace.*) What do you expect me to do? Put the knife in her neck as she handed it to me?

DOUGLAS. (*Moving chair* D. L.) Exactly! What can either of us be expected to do? Neither of us will be able to lay a hand on her.

FRANCIS. There must be a way. There must be a way. We aren't so easily defeated. Douglas! There is a way! A way which will finish her as swiftly and neatly as a blow in the back, and it will look more like an accident. (*Crossing quickly* L. *to bell, which he pulls.*)

DOUGLAS. What do you want Harris for? He'll be in his bed by now.

FRANCIS. Not he. (*He continues to ring.* HARRIS *comes in* U. R. *Neither man expects him at that entrance.*)

HARRIS. What is it, sir? (*The brothers spin round and look at him from* D. L.)

FRANCIS. Harris, Mr. Douglas and I are appalled by the state of the cellars. The passages are overrun with rats.

HARRIS. (*Above fireplace.*) I know that, sir.

FRANCIS. We cannot have these vermin in the place.

HARRIS. (*Moving* C.) No, sir.

FRANCIS. We have decided to get rid of them.

HARRIS. Yes, sir.

DOUGLAS. Yes, Harris, a black rat frightened Miss Oberon. We cannot have that.

HARRIS. No, sir.

FRANCIS. To-morrow morning, Harris, get us some poison.

HARRIS. Arsenic, sir, or strychnine?

DOUGLAS. It doesn't matter, Harris, anything will do.

HARRIS. Very good, sir.

DOUGLAS. What a master-stroke, old boy. Why didn't we think of that before? Good night, Harris.

HARRIS. Good night, sir. Good night. (*He is going upstairs.*)

CURTAIN

ACT II

SCENE 2

A sunny afternoon: the following day. TONI *is singing happily to herself as she arranges some flowers in a vase.* HARRIS *enters* D. L. *and crosses to sideboard.*

TONI. (U. C. *at table.*) Lovely afternoon, isn't it, Harris?

HARRIS. It is indeed, miss.

TONI. The garden is a mass of colour. I have never seen it looking so exquisite.

HARRIS. Yes, miss. (U. C.) Spring is always a delightful season here.

TONI. I like to think we are to look forward to many more such springs, Harris.

HARRIS. I am sure we are, miss.

TONI. What have you there?

HARRIS. Commissions for Mr. Francis and Mr. Douglas from the village.

TONI. Do you know where they are?

HARRIS. No, miss. I will leave them here, miss, if I may. (*Puts two little white paper bags on the table.*)

TONI. Yes, it's very beautiful. But there's something fleeting about the loveliness of spring. It almost makes me sad.

HARRIS. I am sure there is no need for that, miss.

TONI. An irrational sadness, Harris. Or perhaps we sense the transience of all things, including our poor selves, in the swift life of spring.

HARRIS. The summer and autumn have their own qualities, miss.

TONI. You are right, Harris. I must change the flowers in the library. (*She goes out U. R.*)

(HARRIS *continues to busy himself in the room.* DOUGLAS *enters* D. L. *He is limping and walks with a stick.*)

HARRIS. Excuse me, sir, but the apothecary wished me to mention that there is an outstanding account.

DOUGLAS. What the devil does he mean? (*Crossing to table.*) Haven't we been dealing with him for three hundred and fifty years? What does he want to mention his account for now?

HARRIS. Yes, sir. I told him as much.

DOUGLAS. This mine? (*Picks up one packet from table. The audience sees it clearly.*)

HARRIS. (*At fireplace.*) Yes, sir.

DOUGLAS. Humph! (*Puts the little white packet in his*

pocket and goes out D. L. HARRIS *continues to busy himself at fireplace.* TONI *re-enters* U. R.)

TONI. The library looks much better, now.

HARRIS. A few flowers make a lot of difference, miss. I remember in the days of your great-grandmother, the whole house was alive with them. The rooms were festooned and garlanded; roses, pinks, azaleas, tulips. It was like the tides of the sea, miss, the flowers which came tumbling in here. With each changing season, we had a fresh invasion of perfume and yellows and blues.

TONI. And so we shall again, Harris.

HARRIS. I have no doubt of it, miss.

TONI. I would like to bring in some blossom.

HARRIS. She used to bring in blossom, and a branch broken by her hand didn't die till we had tasted the fruit.

TONI. Then we can but try. (*Exit to garden* U. R. HARRIS *continues working near to table.* FRANCIS *enters from stairs and approaches table.*)

FRANCIS. Mr. Douglas, I take it, has already received his packet?

HARRIS. Five minutes ago, sir. (*Hands* FRANCIS *packet.*)

FRANCIS. Thank you, Harris. Have you seen Miss Oberon?

HARRIS. She is in the garden, sir.

FRANCIS. Is she busy?

HARRIS. She is plucking blossom, I fancy, sir. (*Both are standing* U. S. C. *at table.*)

FRANCIS. Whatever for?

HARRIS. She is decking the house with flowers, sir.

FRANCIS. Wreaths and bouquets! (*Crossing to foot of stairs.*)

HARRIS. Beg pardon, sir?

FRANCIS. How prophetic! (*Exit, tossing his packet in his hand as he walks upstairs.* HARRIS *continues to work.* TONI *comes in* U. R. *with twigs of blossom.*)

TONI. Where do you think I should put these, Harris?

HARRIS. Your great-grandmother always put them in the banquet hall.

TONI. Then we cannot do better. (*Exit* D. L. HARRIS *works.* DOUGLAS *enters* D. L. *with a parcel, tied and stamped.*)

DOUGLAS. I'm putting this on the hall table, Harris. See it isn't touched.

HARRIS. Very good, sir. Is it to be collected by the postman?

DOUGLAS. Mind your own business, Harris. (*Exit* U. R. *into the hall. In a second he returns and limps across the stage.*) And if anyone wants me, I'll be in the music room overlooking the drive. (*Exit* D. L. HARRIS *continues working.* TONI *enters* D. L.)

TONI. (*To sofa,* C.) You are quite right, Harris. The banquet hall has lost its gloomy shadows, and a pale bundle of leaves has made it a friendlier place.

HARRIS. (L. *of sofa.*) There was a time, miss—but why am I thinking of it?

TONI. (*Kneels on sofa.*) Tell me, Harris. I should like to hear.

HARRIS. (C., *above sofa.*) There was music and dancing in the big hall in the old days. There was colour and movement, and none of the sombre grey which has crept over the house since I was a boy.

TONI. Harris, I'll tell you a secret. I'm going to have the place redecorated. A spring-clean from head to foot, and you'll no longer be the only servant in the house, but the butler at the head of his staff.

HARRIS. Miss Oberon!

TONI. The walls will be papered and painted anew. The glass will sparkle and the fresh air will blow through the empty rooms.

HARRIS. And the cellars, miss? Will you be having those bricked up?

TONI. No, Harris, we'll keep them as they are, for you never know when they might be useful.

HARRIS. I cannot wait to see it begin, miss. When is it to be?

TONI. When I come back again.

HARRIS. Then you're going away?

TONI. I can't stay here for ever. This was a visit. I merely came to meet my cousins, and see the estate. Next time . . .

HARRIS. When will that be, miss?

TONI. I shall not come again unless I am invited.

HARRIS. (*Coming forward conspiratorially.*) I did not want to say this, Miss Oberon, but I feel you ought to know— (*They do not see* FRANCIS *who is coming quietly downstairs.*)

FRANCIS. (*Speaking from stairs.*) Harris, would you bring Miss Oberon and myself afternoon tea?

HARRIS. (*Unshaken.*) Very good, sir. (*Exit* D. L.)

FRANCIS. He's a talkative fellow.

TONI. I find him fascinating. He worships this house. It's his religion.

FRANCIS. (*Going to fireplace.*) It exercises a charm over a number of people, but Harris permits himself a certain amount of ostentatious enthusiasm.

TONI. It's true he is unable to disguise his emotions as we do, Francis.

FRANCIS. The display of emotion has always struck me as a little ill-mannered.

TONI. I agree. And how we do disguise our thoughts and feelings. What stranger seeing us would have guessed my fears when I arrived here that first evening? What stranger could have guessed your resentment?

FRANCIS. (*Still standing at fireplace.*) Cousin Toni—

TONI. Do not protest, Francis. It is true, I had hoped for so much from this visit. I was to meet my only relations, to see our ancestral home. It was an ordeal for me, but I don't believe you would have guessed from my face.

FRANCIS. To tell the truth, I did not.

TONI. How you and Douglas must have hated me.

FRANCIS. You exaggerate.

TONI. You have forgotten, perhaps, as friendship and

confidence have grown between us. Francis, can you keep a secret? (*Rising from sofa pensively.*)

FRANCIS. You know you can trust me. (*She is moving away.*)

TONI. I am in love.

FRANCIS. Do I know the man?

TONI. (*Moving round towards fireplace.*) I am in love with two men and a house.

FRANCIS. I see.

TONI. What are you thinking?

FRANCIS. It occurred to me, just a sudden thought, that I had been nearer the mark than my brother. Before you came, Douglas and I discussed you. What were you going to be like? On reflection I seem to have been the more accurate.

TONI. (*Crossing U. C. away from FRANCIS.*) I am not surprised. I, too, guessed you would be as you are. But I had not expected anyone quite like Douglas.

FRANCIS. Don't you like him?

TONI. It isn't that. He's a little different from us, that's all.

FRANCIS. Us? (*Crossing U. C. after her.*)

TONI. You and me.

FRANCIS. Do you mean . . . ?

TONI. Let us not dwell on little differences. Douglas is as he is: and we are as we are.

FRANCIS. That, at least, is incontestable.

TONI. Dear Francis! If only I could have one swift glimpse into your heart.

FRANCIS. You might find some very surprising things.

TONI. But not unwelcome, I am sure.

FRANCIS. I hope not.

TONI. (D. C. *to back of sofa.*) Perhaps you think it immodest of me to be so frank, but never before have I met anyone so like myself, with whom I felt so much at home.

FRANCIS. Do you mean me, cousin Toni? (*Crossing after her to behind sofa.*)

TONI. You know I do. With you I no longer need to

pretend. I am content that you should know the truth, my faults and weaknesses.

FRANCIS. My dear Toni . . .

TONI. I am content to place my care and safety in your hands.

FRANCIS. Do you realise what you are saying?

TONI. (*Sitting on sofa.*) Of course. After all, it's only to be expected I should feel like this. You are my cousin.

FRANCIS. But we are only distant cousins, very distant; several times removed.

TONI. There seems to be such a strong tie holding us together, and what else could it be? (*She looks at him innocently.*)

FRANCIS. (*At back of sofa.*) I don't know. I must think. You don't seem to realise what you have been implying. Why, you have practically suggested, well, that you love me.

TONI. But my dear Francis, I do love you. I told you so.

FRANCIS. You did?

TONI. I said I loved two men.

FRANCIS. Two?

TONI. You and Douglas.

FRANCIS. Oh, Douglas! (*Crossing* U. C. *in exasperation.*)

(HARRIS *enters* D. L. *with a silver tray, cups, plates and tea.* TONI *remains sitting* R. *on sofa.*)

HARRIS. Where would you like it, sir?

FRANCIS. Ah, the tea. I was forgetting. Put it over there, Harris. (*Indicating table* U. S. C.)

HARRIS. Very good, sir. Will you pour, Miss Oberon?

FRANCIS. (*Moving to table.*) That's all right, Harris. Don't get up, Toni. I will pour it out.

TONI. Thank you.

HARRIS. Would you not like me to do it, sir?

FRANCIS. No, Harris, I should not.

HARRIS. Very good, sir.

FRANCIS. That will be all, Harris. You may go. What are you hanging about for?

HARRIS. I thought you might like me to hand Miss Oberon her tea.

FRANCIS. No, Harris, I can manage perfectly, thank you. .

HARRIS. Yes, sir. (*Exit* D. L.)

FRANCIS. Does he think me incapable of pouring a cup of tea without splashing the saucer?

TONI. He likes to look after us.

FRANCIS. Then it's time he realised we are no longer children. Sugar? (FRANCIS *is pouring out the tea. As he puts in sugar he pours in the contents of a packet he takes from his pocket. This is done very visibly, tapping the packet a few inches above the cup, and watching with pleasure the mixture trickle into the cup.*)

TONI. Yes, please. Two lumps. Harris will have known you since you were boys? (TONI *does not once turn her head to watch him.*)

FRANCIS. He practically brought us up. Milk?

TONI. A little.

FRANCIS. China or Indian?

TONI. Indian.

FRANCIS. Weak or strong?

TONI. (*Turning to him.*) Weak, please, and I said two lumps, not three.

FRANCIS. I only put in two.

TONI. I'm sorry. I thought I saw you put in three.

FRANCIS. (*Crossing with teacup above sofa.*) There. I hope that's how you like it. Petits four? (*Offers plate.*)

TONI. No, thank you. Is Douglas not coming to tea?

FRANCIS. (*Bringing little stool from behind sofa as table for* TONI.) I think he may be late to-day. (*Moving round to fireplace with his own cup of tea.*)

TONI. It is rather nice, only the two of us. I watched you pouring out.

FRANCIS. Why? (*Turning round with suspicion.*)

TONI. You looked so sweet. It made me rather wish

there were only you and me. That we would never be disturbed. Just quietly, cosily, living here and drinking tea.

FRANCIS. (*Sitting* D. L. *at fireplace.*) Cousin Toni, something you said this afternoon gives me courage to speak.

TONI. Yes, Francis?

FRANCIS. Even before I ever saw you, I had evolved a special feeling for you. I had a strange premonition. I told my brother of it.

TONI. What was it, Francis?

FRANCIS. For some unaccountable reason I felt we would mean rather much to each other. Never before had I thought of marriage.

TONI. Oh, Francis. The moment I saw you I knew . . . but I can't tell you this. (*Stirs her tea.*)

FRANCIS. Do, Toni. Please do. So much depends on it. (*She is about to drink.*) No, no, don't drink your tea yet. Do try a petit four. Please tell me. What did you think?

TONI. That you . . . you . . .

FRANCIS. Yes? Yes? Is there a chance that you care for me in a special way?

TONI. Yes. (*Lifts her cup to drink.*)

FRANCIS. (*Getting up abruptly, crossing to* TONI *and taking cup.*) Stop! I believe I did put three lumps of sugar in that tea. I'll pour you another cup. (*He takes the cup up to table, pours it away, and fills it again from the teapot. As he takes her cup, he gives her his, which* TONI *holds until* FRANCIS *comes back with fresh cup.*) Two lumps, Indian, weak. I shall never forget how you like your tea.

TONI. Oh, Francis, if it were not for this strange feeling about Douglas.

FRANCIS. (*He is about to take teacup to her: stops in alarm.*) Douglas! (*Looks with dawning regret at the tea he has poured away.*)

TONI. If he didn't exist, I could be so sure of my feeling for you.

FRANCIS. Has Douglas been very friendly with you when I wasn't here? (*Coming* D. R. *to sofa back.*)

TONI. A little. I was so sorry for him when he was hurt. I felt I was to blame. And it's so easy for Douglas to make his presence felt in subtle ways. (*Taking teacup and handing back the other one.*)

FRANCIS. Is it, indeed?

TONI. Don't be cross with him. It's all my fault. I'm getting so confused. For whom do I really care? Do either of you care for me? (*Stirring tea.*)

FRANCIS. You know I do, Toni.

TONI. I hope so. (*Drinking.*) This is delicious tea.

FRANCIS. They say it's better from the second cup.

(FRANCIS *begins to laugh. The laugh grows.* TONI *joins in merrily.* DOUGLAS *enters from* D. L. *He is looking at them in amazement.* FRANCIS *returns the look coldly.*)

TONI. Here you are, Douglas. I wondered when you were coming to tea.

DOUGLAS. You seem to be enjoying yourselves. (*Crossing towards them as far as* C.)

FRANCIS. Is that unusual?

DOUGLAS. What was the joke?

FRANCIS. (*Crossing to fireplace.*) Is it so strange to see us laugh, that we must have a post-mortem on it?

DOUGLAS. A very apt metaphor.

TONI. Let me pour you some tea. You will have a cup? (*Rising and crossing below sofa to table with tea.*)

DOUGLAS. Is Francis drinking?

FRANCIS. Of course I am.

DOUGLAS. Very well, I will.

TONI. How do you like it?

DOUGLAS. With a slice of lemon and sugar, please . . . if Francis recommends both the lemon and the sugar.

FRANCIS. Why shouldn't I? What an idiotic thing to say. Excuse me, Toni, I shall be in my room as long as Douglas is going to talk nonsense. (*Goes upstairs.*)

TONI. What's the matter with him?

DOUGLAS. Francis was always a temperamental boy. (*Sits on sofa.*)

TONI. I'm sorry to hear that. Petits fours?

DOUGLAS. No, thanks. They are too sweet for me.

TONI. You don't like sweet things, do you? (*Sits on stool beside sofa; opposite* DOUGLAS, *looking up at him.*)

DOUGLAS. Not much.

TONI. In fact you'd rather have things rough and sour. I've noticed that about you.

DOUGLAS. Have you?

TONI. You like to do things the hard and dangerous way.

DOUGLAS. What are you driving at?

TONI. Don't look alarmed. Drink your tea.

DOUGLAS. Just what have you found out from Francis?

TONI. Nothing that would interest you.

DOUGLAS. Anything about us?

TONI. In a way.

DOUGLAS. (*Grabbing her wrist.*) Come on. Out with it. What have you wangled out of him?

TONI. Douglas, you're hurting my wrist.

DOUGLAS. What did he tell you?

TONI. Only that he was in love with me. (DOUGLAS *lets her wrist fall. He can hardly believe his ears.*)

DOUGLAS. (*Rising.*) In love with you!

TONI. Is there anything so extraordinary in that?

DOUGLAS. I don't believe it.

TONI. You're very rude. And you haven't apologized for hurting my wrist.

DOUGLAS. (*Crossing behind sofa.*) He surely can't . . . I don't believe Francis would . . . (*But he is bewildered and talking to himself.*)

TONI. There's no need to be so amazed because your brother likes me. I don't expect you to behave the same way, knowing how unattractive you find me.

DOUGLAS. What gave you that idea?

TONI. Well, Francis is always so polite to me when

you aren't here. He goes out of his way to show me a certain amount of kindliness and attention.

DOUGLAS. (*Crossing to* TONI *at fireplace.*) Tell me more. What else does my brother do?

TONI. I won't tell you, if you're going to be horrid. Oh, Douglas, what have I done that makes you hate me so?

DOUGLAS. You are quite wrong, Toni. I am angry with Francis because, if anything, I like you more than he does, and I am annoyed to think he has gone behind my back.

TONI. I wouldn't have taken him seriously, Douglas, if I had known this.

DOUGLAS. Did you encourage him?

TONI. I did a little, but that was because I didn't know you'd even noticed me.

DOUGLAS. Cousin Toni, you are seldom out of my thoughts.

TONI. Douglas! (*There is no saying what show of affection there might have been, but* HARRIS *enters* D. L.)

DOUGLAS. What is it, Harris?

HARRIS. The postman, sir. (*He is going* U. R. *to the front door.*)

DOUGLAS. That's all right. I'll go.

HARRIS. Do not disturb yourself, sir.

DOUGLAS. That's all right, Harris. I will go. (DOUGLAS *goes* U. R. *into the hall and returns immediately with letters and his parcel.*) Two letters for Francis, and a parcel . . . What do you want, Harris?

HARRIS. Nothing, sir.

DOUGLAS. Then you may go.

HARRIS. Yes, sir. (*Exit* D. L.)

DOUGLAS. And a parcel for me. Let us see what it is. (*Going* D. R. *It is obviously the parcel which* DOUGLAS *had put in the hall himself. He begins to unwrap it.*)

TONI. What a lovely box of chocolates!

DOUGLAS. And just to prove that I'm always thinking of you . . . (*He hands her a card from the box.*)

TONI. (*Reading.*) "With love to Toni." Douglas, how sweet of you. How charming. I don't know what to say. (*Kneeling on chair above fireplace.*)

DOUGLAS. I hope you like them. They have been specially made.

TONI. They look divine.

DOUGLAS. Try one and see. (*He offers her the box.*)

TONI. Thanks, I will.

DOUGLAS. No, no. Not those. They are hard.

TONI. And these?

DOUGLAS. They are toffee centres. You prefer creams.

TONI. How did you know?

DOUGLAS. I think I know all about you.

TONI. Which are the creams?

DOUGLAS. Those round ones at the end.

TONI. (*Taking one.*) How clever you are, Douglas. (*Standing.*) You know all about the insides of chocolates by their shape. I'll take it when we finish tea. (*She puts the chocolate down in her saucer.*)

DOUGLAS. I've finished mine.

TONI. Would you like more?

DOUGLAS. No, thanks.

TONI. A chocolate?

DOUGLAS. I never touch them.

TONI. I think I'll have a second cup of tea. (*Crosses below sofa to tea table.*)

DOUGLAS. Oh, very well. (*He tries to hide his annoyance while she pours it out. As she does so, TONI asks him thoughtfully:*)

TONI. Would you be angry, Douglas, if Francis married me?

DOUGLAS. So that's his game.

TONI. Would it mean anything to you?

DOUGLAS. You know perfectly well it would. Good heavens, Toni, you mustn't throw yourself away on him.

TONI. I told him I couldn't make up my mind.

DOUGLAS. What did he say to that?

TONI. He said he had planned to marry me even before I came to stay.

DOUGLAS. (*Moving up to* TONI.) He's a futile bungler. A hopeless, effete fellow, who would bore you in less than a fortnight.

TONI. He can be so sweet.

DOUGLAS. Sweet! Is that the quality you ask of a man?

TONI. I don't have much choice. Francis loves me; I think I love him.

DOUGLAS. You only think?

TONI. (*Moving with teacup* D. R. *to fireplace.*) I told him I could be sure if it were not for you.

DOUGLAS. What difference do I make?

TONI. I deceived myself into believing that he could be everything, and then the sight of you, or even the thought, and then I'm not so sure.

DOUGLAS. Toni. If that's true . . . If you really mean . . . I promise you . . .

TONI. Oh, Douglas, if only I could be certain. (*Puts cup down.*)

DOUGLAS. You can be.

TONI. But what about Francis?

DOUGLAS. (*Moving* D. R. *to* TONI *at fireplace.*) To the devil with Francis.

TONI. If it were not for the thought of him . . . if he did not exist, I know I could be so happy with you.

DOUGLAS. Forget him.

TONI. I can't.

DOUGLAS. No? (*Throwing down his walking stick, he takes her roughly in his arms and kisses her. She melts into his embrace.* FRANCIS *is coming down stairs, sees them, and then slowly backs up stairs again, unseen by them.*)

TONI. Oh, Douglas, let me go. I cannot think.

DOUGLAS. Very well, Toni. Think. Take your time. Decide between my brother and me. I shall be waiting.

TONI. (*Crossing behind sofa to tea table.*) Give me a day or two. I hesitate to hurt his pride. (*She is going, when she remembers her chocolate.*) Oh, my chocolate! (*She turns to pick it up.*)

DOUGLAS. Don't touch that. (*He almost shouts, as he takes it from her.*)

TONI. Why?

DOUGLAS. It has melted against your cup.

TONI. (D. C., *above sofa.*) I must go, Douglas. You have ruffled my hair, and smudged my face.

DOUGLAS. You look divine. But go, by all means, if you promise to return.

TONI. I will. (*Exit up stairs.*)

(DOUGLAS *picks up the chocolate, takes it and the box to the fireplace and throws them in. There he watches them burn, raking them over with his stick. As he does so,* FRANCIS *comes down stairs, with a quick look over his shoulder to where he has obviously seen* TONI *pass.*)

FRANCIS. Well, brother, what success have you had?

DOUGLAS. The same amount as you had yourself.

FRANCIS. I was unlucky. She had her eye on me.

DOUGLAS. And you had your eye on her, too, it seems.

FRANCIS. I don't follow you.

DOUGLAS. No? I thought you were going to end this story with a cup of tea.

FRANCIS. And you were going to make sure of her with a box of chocolates.

DOUGLAS. There they are. (*Gestures contemptuously to fireplace beside him.*)

FRANCIS. You have destroyed them?

DOUGLAS. What did you do with your cup of tea?

FRANCIS. Poured it away.

DOUGLAS. I see. A change of heart.

FRANCIS. (*Crosses to* C.) Not at all. It didn't seem the moment, that was all.

DOUGLAS. Perhaps you're right. Perhaps the moment is past, and we ought to be considering another plan, like a stab in the back.

FRANCIS. (*Moving* L.) I do not understand you, Douglas, but I take it you, too, have failed.

DOUGLAS. I have failed in one venture, but in another I like to think I have had some success.

FRANCIS. (L.) I do believe you have, Douglas. (*Swinging round on* DOUGLAS.) But perhaps the race is not yet over, and the fight not won.

DOUGLAS. (*Moves from fireplace to back of sofa.*) From now on, brother, I know which way to turn, and I shall guard against another accident.

FRANCIS. (*Comes to back of sofa* L.) And I, too, shall be prepared for anyone who tries to steal a march.

DOUGLAS. We shall see. It is a rare thing to know for the first time who one's enemy is, and to prepare to deal with him.

FRANCIS. The pleasure is mutual, and preparation can be a two-handed thing. (HARRIS *enters* D. L.)

HARRIS. Did you call, sir?

FRANCIS. No, we did not, Harris. (*Exit* U. R., *barely suppressing his rage.*)

DOUGLAS. Yes, we did, Harris. Take away the tea. (*He storms off stage* D. L.)

HARRIS. Very good, sir. (*He begins to collect the cups and put them on the tray. Then he looks at the burnt chocolates in the grate, and, still inscrutable, at the slop basin of tea on the table. While he is doing so,* TONI *enters, coming down stairs—innocent as ever.*)

TONI. (*Speaking at foot of stairs—looking round room.*) Where are my cousins, Harris?

HARRIS. (C.) They went their several ways, miss.

TONI. Oh! (*There is quite a long, significant pause. She moves towards fireplace.*)

HARRIS. If I may be allowed to say so, miss, I have never seen them at variance before. This is the first time anyone has divided them.

TONI. (*Blandly.*) Are they divided, Harris?

HARRIS. If I may be permitted an opinion, miss, there is between them just the thin end of a wedge, a breath of suspicion, of jealousy, doubt.

TONI. (*At fireplace.*) You say some very amusing things, Harris. I never understand what you mean.

HARRIS. Very good, miss. Very good, miss, (*Picks up tray to go* L., *stopping* L. C.) so long as they don't catch you out.

TONI. (*There is a quiet strength and confidence in her voice as she says softly:*) They won't catch me, Harris.

HARRIS. I hope not, miss.

CURTAIN

ACT III

The same evening: DOUGLAS, R., *and* FRANCIS, L., *are
sitting over the remnants of dinner as they were in
Act I. As the curtain goes up* HARRIS *enters* D. L.
The stage is set as in Act I, Scene 1, with table D. C.

HARRIS. (*To* FRANCIS.) Port, sir?

FRANCIS. Brandy.

HARRIS. (*To* DOUGLAS.) Brandy, sir?

DOUGLAS. Port. (HARRIS *pours and goes out* D. L.,
leaving decanters on the sideboard.)

FRANCIS. But for your interference, I could have married her.

DOUGLAS. Don't make a fool of yourself. She isn't interested in you.

FRANCIS. Every chance we have had you have thrown away.

DOUGLAS. And what have you achieved?

FRANCIS. Murder was your idea. I left it to you. You
bungled the business in the cellar, and botched the attempt to throttle the girl.

DOUGLAS. I seem to remember a knife slipping from
your nerveless hand on the stairs.

FRANCIS. I repeat, murder was your affair. I suggested
marriage from the first, and I could succeed in it but for
this futile attitude of yours.

DOUGLAS. That is an insulting thing to say.

FRANCIS. Take it as you please. It was my idea. I, or
no one, will marry the girl.

DOUGLAS. If you insist in making a deadlock out of
the affair . . .

FRANCIS. It is you, confound you . . .

DOUGLAS. Don't excite yourself, brother.

FRANCIS. To see you ruining our chances of laying
our hands on this wealth! That fortune could be ours by
now.

74

DOUGLAS. Whose?

FRANCIS. Yours and mine. Have you any reason to question it?

DOUGLAS. I will not give you cause for a grievance.

FRANCIS. You have done that already, and you shall pay for it. Only one of us can profit from cousin Toni now.

DOUGLAS. I take that as a friendly warning, brother. (TONI *comes down stairs. The men rise.*)

TONI. The withdrawing-room is chilly this evening, Douglas. Would you be good enough to ask Harris to serve coffee here.

DOUGLAS. Of course. (*Exit* D. L.)

TONI. This is the only warm room in the house. (*Goes to fireplace and warms her hands.*)

FRANCIS. Toni! (*He crosses to her, whispering urgently.*) There is something I must tell you. I have hesitated about warning you before, as I did not want to turn you against Douglas. My brother, I regret to say, is not all he seems.

TONI. Whatever can be wrong with him?

FRANCIS. He worships wealth, and feels he still owns this place. There is no knowing the lengths he may go to, to make sure it remains his. He is a dangerous man.

TONI. Douglas?

FRANCIS. I was shocked myself when I discovered it. I don't think you're safe here, Toni. I'm going to do my best to get you away.

TONI. You're going to look after me?

FRANCIS. Of course. I will get you out of his reach first. Don't forget I have not yet given up hope that one day you will really care for me.

TONI. It must have hurt you to tell me this, for I know how closely you are bound to your brother.

FRANCIS. (*Moves* R. *of table.*) No longer. When I found out that I could not trust him, I cut him out of my confidence.

TONI. Does he know?

FRANCIS. He guesses. That's what makes it so urgent

to act at once. To-night I shall get you away. (*Enter* DOUGLAS D. L.)

DOUGLAS. Harris is bringing the coffee.

TONI. Thank you, Douglas.

DOUGLAS. (L. *of table*.) I think he wants to speak to you in private, Francis.

FRANCIS. Harris wants to speak to me? How most extraordinary. Excuse me. (*Exits* D. L. *after giving* DOUGLAS *a sharp look*.)

DOUGLAS. (*Crossing to* TONI R.) I said that to get him out of the way. Listen, Toni. Have nothing to do with him. He's trying to marry you to get hold of your money.

TONI. (*Moving to* DOUGLAS.) To get my money?

DOUGLAS. He has asked you to marry him, hasn't he?

TONI. But he loves me.

DOUGLAS. He loves only himself. He is a grasping, vindictive devil, who won't share a penny he hasn't got to.

TONI. What shall I do?

DOUGLAS. You won't marry him, will you?

TONI. After what you've told me! I shall be terrified now, with Francis here.

DOUGLAS. Don't worry. I think we might be able to get him out of the way. (*Enter* FRANCIS *angrily* D. L.)

FRANCIS. What sort of a joke was that? You knew damn well Harris didn't want to see me.

DOUGLAS. Indeed? My mistake.

FRANCIS. Has he been upsetting you, Toni?

DOUGLAS. What the devil do you mean by that?

FRANCIS. You should know.

TONI. Francis! Douglas! Please! (*Sits at chair* C. *of table*.)

FRANCIS. I beg your pardon.

DOUGLAS. I do apologise. (*They are standing on either side of her and bow as they apologise, then sit down rigidly at different ends of the table*.)

TONI. What can the matter be? You used to be such

good friends. What has happened? You quarrel over the slightest thing. (*The BELL rings at the outer door.*)

DOUGLAS. I'll see who it is. As a matter of fact I could do with a breath of fresh air. (*Exit U. R.*)

FRANCIS. (*Rising angrily.*) You see how insolent he is.

TONI. Try and put up with it. It won't be for long.

FRANCIS. You are right there. I don't think we shall be troubled much more with Douglas. You never drink port, do you, Toni? (*Crossing to sideboard, L.*)

TONI. Never, thank you.

FRANCIS. I thought not. (*He pours a glass of brandy. He looks at her, but TONI does not appear to be watching him. He taps his packet of poison into the port decanter, and then joins her with his drink.*) Nor will you join me in a brandy, I suppose?

TONI. No, thank you. (*Enter DOUGLAS U. R.*)

DOUGLAS. It's that journalist again. She's going back to town. She wants to see you first.

TONI. (*Getting up.*) Press-day! I'd quite forgotten. Where is she?

DOUGLAS. In the hall. (*Exit TONI, U. R. FRANCIS gives DOUGLAS a cool look.*)

FRANCIS. You will, of course, excuse me? (*Exit D. L. DOUGLAS looks after him.*)

DOUGLAS. I will do more than excuse you, brother.

(*Exit DOUGLAS hurriedly upstairs as TONI and MISS RICHARDS enter U. R.*)

TONI. (*Moving in R. C.*) Come in. My cousins won't eat you. Why, they have gone! (*Reaching MS. from mantelpiece.*) Here is your article. Thank you so much for letting me read it. I changed only one or two things.

MISS RICHARDS. Do you think they object to my calling?

TONI. My cousins? No. It isn't that, Miss Richards. It's much worse. They have had a dreadful quarrel.

MISS RICHARDS. But they are such good friends!

TONI. They were. That's what makes it all the worse. Now they are at daggers drawn.

Miss Richards. What about?

Toni. Me.

Miss Richards. You?

Toni. They're at each other's throats. I'm so terrified they'll do each other an injury.

Miss Richards. And in such a short time!

Toni. I feel I ought to go away.

Miss Richards. Would that help?

Toni. They might realise I wasn't worth fighting over.

Miss Richards. Are they fighting?

Toni. At this very instant, for all we know, Miss Richards, they might be hacking one another to pieces.

Miss Richards. Oh!

Toni. So, you see, you really are my only chance.

Miss Richards. What can I do?

Toni. You are going back to town to-night?

Miss Richards. Yes.

Toni. Then first thing to-morrow morning, please, please, go to this address. (*Scribbles address.*) They are the Oberon solicitors. Describe how violent my cousins have become. Say I cannot manage them any longer. I need help.

Miss Richards. Why haven't you 'phoned?

Toni. Wherever I go, Douglas or Francis are at my heels.

Miss Richards. They follow you? Why?

Toni. Each is so frightened I should elope with the other.

Miss Richards. Suppose they get out of hand? Will to-morrow morning be soon enough?

Toni. I think I can keep them apart until then.

Miss Richards. As you think best.

Toni. (*Crossing to sideboard* L., *picking up camera and hand-bag. Moving back to* R. C. *table.*) You are so understanding, Miss Richards. I have your camera here. It was very useful. I took several snaps of the house, but only one came out. (*Handing* Miss Richards *a photograph out of hand-bag.*)

Miss Richards. (*Peering at it.*) Which room is this?

TONI. The cellars. Taken after the accident, of course. (*Points to photo.*) Look at the broken beams and the crumbling walls.

MISS RICHARDS. What's this rope tied across like a rabbit snare?

TONI. Now, do you know, I hadn't noticed it. Please keep that copy for your magazine. I have another here.

MISS RICHARDS. Where was this developed?

TONI. In the village, by the chemist. While I was there I settled a very long-standing debt. (TONI *takes a very old scroll of paper from her bag.*)

MISS RICHARDS. A very ancient document.

TONI. It seems the family have always dealt there and always failed to pay. I settled the account. It's quite intriguing. It shows there have been rats in the house since the beginning; and we have tried hard to get rid of them. For centuries now, our purchases have been nothing but cocaine, hashish and bhang.

MISS RICHARDS. Whatever is that?

TONI. Poison, Miss Richards. Ratbane, henbane, deadly nightshade . . .

MISS RICHARDS. Why, that's enough to exterminate an army.

TONI. The rats in this house seem to have survived miraculously, don't you think? (*Enter* HARRIS D. L. *with coffee.*)

HARRIS. Your coffee, miss. (*Puts coffee on table.*)

TONI. Won't you stay for a cup?

MISS RICHARDS. (*With an uncertain glance at the coffee.*) If you don't mind, I'd rather not. (*Moving* U. R.)

TONI. I feel much happier now, knowing my commission is in such safe hands.

MISS RICHARDS. Good night.

TONI. Harris, show Miss Richards out. Good night.

(*Exeunt* HARRIS *and* MISS RICHARDS U. R. TONI *sits at table and pours out her coffee.* HARRIS *re-enters* U. R.)

HARRIS. Will that be all, miss?

TONI. I will say good-bye to you now, Harris.

HARRIS. I thought as much, miss.

TONI. You are observant.

HARRIS. I see a good deal of what goes on, miss. I will prepare your room, and look forward to an early return.

TONI. A week or so, Harris. Did you guess that also?

HARRIS. Yes, miss. And then we will have the whole house painted anew; colour and laughter . . . but it's sad that things should have to be like this. If only they were not so arbitrary. I've seen them grow up. It's their unconciliatory nature. They won't deviate. They won't bend, or give in. They will break first.

TONI. Yes, Harris, they will break. Otherwise I'd never be very safe, would I, Harris?

HARRIS. I'm afraid you wouldn't, miss. (DOUGLAS *comes down the stairs.*)

TONI. You're just in time for your coffee. White?

DOUGLAS. Black.

TONI. Is Francis coming?

DOUGLAS. I have no idea.

HARRIS. Will that be all, miss?

TONI. Yes, thank you, Harris. (*Exit* HARRIS D. L.)

DOUGLAS. Thank you. (*Takes his coffee from her across to the sideboard where are the wine decanters.*) You never drink brandy, do you, Toni?

TONI. No, Douglas. Brandy does not agree with me.

DOUGLAS. I take port myself. (*He gives her a quick look but she does not appear to notice him. He lets the contents of his packet of poison drop gently into the brandy decanter, shaking it round to dissolve it. Sips coffee calmly.*) Delicious coffee. You haven't forgotten what I said?

TONI. Not for a moment.

DOUGLAS. Good. I'll let you know if he . . . (*Enter* FRANCIS D. L.)

TONI. Ah, Francis. Coffee is here. Black?

FRANCIS. White.

TONI. How nice and cosy this is. Don't you think we

might sit and have coffee, happily, as we used to do when I first came?

FRANCIS. Unfortunately there have been some changes since then.

DOUGLAS. One or two very unpleasant discoveries. (*They are glaring at each other.*)

TONI. Why don't you have a drink together and be friends?

FRANCIS. That's the last thing I would do.

TONI. If you're not going to be pleasant to each other you leave me with only one thing to do. You make me feel I am to blame. I am going to pack my things. (*Rises.*) If you have reached a saner state of mind when I come down, I'll stay. If not, I promise you I'll go to-night.

FRANCIS. (*Closing in on* TONI, L. *side of table.*) Do go, Toni. Go to-night. I will accompany you.

DOUGLAS. (*Moving in* R. *side.*) I warned you. Have no truck with him. I'll take you away.

TONI. I'll go myself. (*Turns up to foot of stairs. They both move after her, one on either side.*)

FRANCIS. That's impossible. It must be with one of us.

DOUGLAS. Tell us now, Toni. Who is it to be? (*They stop her on the first step.*)

TONI. Let me collect my things. (*Turns to go upstairs.*)

FRANCIS. No. You must make your choice. Which is it going to be?

TONI. I will let you know when I come down. (*She has managed to keep them in check. She turns and goes up stairs. The two men pace up and down angrily, glaring fiercely at each other, and glancing upstairs.* HARRIS *comes in* D. L.)

FRANCIS. What do you want now, Harris?

HARRIS. Have you finished with the coffee, sir? (*He collects cups at the table. The two men watch him in exasperation.*)

DOUGLAS. Stop fiddling with those damned cups, Harris. Take the coffee and get out.

HARRIS. Very good, sir.

(HARRIS *goes out* D. L. *with the coffee.* DOUGLAS, D. R.,
*by fireplace, throws himself into an armchair, where
he sits biting his nails and glancing upstairs to see
if there is any sign of* TONI. FRANCIS *continues pac-
ing up and down. Then he stops explosively at the
table staring at nothing. He stands there for a few
seconds before his eyes light on* TONI'S *hand-bag,
open, with parchment showing. He looks at it. Something catches his attention. He is apprehensive. He
has seen the chemist's name. He bends down and
picks it up. He smooths it out and reads it. He reads
it again: turns it over. He also takes out photo,
looks at it; looks across at* DOUGLAS *who is still biting ·his nails . . . a deadly calm is settling over*
FRANCIS. *This is the transition. When he speaks to*
DOUGLAS *it is in such a quiet, significant tone that*
DOUGLAS *catches something from it, and he, too, is
influenced by* FRANCIS'S *new, dangerous mood.*)

FRANCIS. Douglas?

DOUGLAS. Yes?

FRANCIS. Have you seen this?

DOUGLAS. What is it?

FRANCIS. It's an account from the chemist in the village. It's receipted. Did you pay for it?

DOUGLAS. No.

FRANCIS. Then who did? And what do you make of
this? (*Moves across to* DOUGLAS *and hands him photo.*)

DOUGLAS. It's a photograph.

FRANCIS. So I see. But do you recognise it?

DOUGLAS. It's the cellar.

FRANCIS. Just what I thought.

DOUGLAS. Why the devil are you showing me these?

FRANCIS. I merely wondered if they suggest to you
what they suggest to me.

DOUGLAS. Who would be interested in our cellar, and
our purchases from the local chemist?

FRANCIS. I couldn't say for certain, but perhaps our cousin . . .

DOUGLAS. Good God! Toni! (*He rises.*)

FRANCIS. I thought so, too.

DOUGLAS. Good heavens, man, don't you see what this means?

FRANCIS. Our dear cousin is not as innocent as she would have us believe.

DOUGLAS. She must have known about the trap, the poison, and about us.

FRANCIS. She played us off, Douglas, one against the other.

DOUGLAS. She's made complete fools of us.

FRANCIS. I have a great admiration for the girl.

DOUGLAS. So have I!

FRANCIS. But we must not allow our admiration to come between us and our plain duty to ourselves.

DOUGLAS. No, of course not.

FRANCIS. How lucky she is still in the house.

DOUGLAS. Why, so she is.

FRANCIS. That's the first time I've seen you smile for a long time, Douglas. (*They look at each other and smile. The partnership is re-established. They are their old selves.*)

DOUGLAS. As we have reached such a deadlock about marriage, don't you think we might reconsider the other method?

FRANCIS. That had also occurred to me. What do you say to a further attempt?

DOUGLAS. I think the occasion is unique.

FRANCIS. You do?

DOUGLAS. My head reels with the ways and means. The silk scarf is as lethal as ever: the paper knife remains as sharp.

FRANCIS. What do you intend?

DOUGLAS. You are squeamish, Francis. Perhaps you will have more stomach for the adventure if I don't go into details.

FRANCIS. Will it look like an accident?

DOUGLAS. It will look like nothing on earth.

FRANCIS. Shall we go and join the lady?

DOUGLAS. Of course. (*With quiet deliberation they go toward the stairs. Together, with an equal deliberate, relentless tread, they go up the first step, when* HARRIS *enters from* D. L.)

HARRIS. Excuse me, sir.

FRANCIS. What is it, Harris?

HARRIS. It's about that murder, sir. (*They both stop as if shot, then slowly turn round towards him.*)

DOUGLAS. What did you say, Harris?

HARRIS. That novel, sir. The one you are writing. You asked me whether to marry or murder the girl.

FRANCIS. Of course, Harris, we remember. You said murder, didn't you?

HARRIS. I did, sir. But I have changed my mind.

DOUGLAS. Why?

HARRIS. Murders are so easily detected nowadays, sir, and the general public do not like their heroes to end on the gallows.

DOUGLAS. Never fear, Harris, we will avoid that.

HARRIS. I am pleased to hear it, sir. I enjoy an exciting plot myself, for a quiet evening in the pantry. But I like a satisfactory finish: something which develops out of the characters themselves. (*Exit* D. L.)

FRANCIS. Harris grows more enigmatic as he gets older.

DOUGLAS. Doddering old fool! Springing it on us like that! Come on. Let's go and get the girl.

FRANCIS. Be quiet. Here she comes. (*They stop and look up.* TONI *is coming down. She is dressed for travel, and carries a little case.* FRANCIS *is at* R. *of stair.* DOUGLAS *on* L. *of stair.*) You were so long, we were quite worried.

DOUGLAS. In fact we were coming to see.

TONI. (*Still on stairs.*) I was packing.

DOUGLAS. The house won't be the same without you. Please do stay.

TONI. No. I have decided. I must go.

DOUGLAS. I suppose we were at fault. (*He walks through* HARRIS'S *archway* D. L. *as he speaks, and we hear him slam home a heavy bolt.*)

TONI. What are you doing?

DOUGLAS. We don't want Harris butting in as we say farewell.

TONI. (*Coming down last stairs.*) What a strange way for Douglas to behave!

FRANCIS. I told you he was dangerous.

TONI. (*Turning to* FRANCIS *on her* R.) Francis, you said you'd help me.

FRANCIS. But you love him, don't you? You're going to marry him, aren't you? When I'm out of the way.

TONI. That isn't true.

DOUGLAS. (D. C.) You have a mercurial heart, Toni. You love me one minute and you don't the next. Is it Francis you are marrying now? (*They are mocking her.*)

FRANCIS. Tell us, Cousin, which is it to be?

TONI. Neither of you.

FRANCIS. (*Moving away a little* D. R. C.) Oh, Toni. Wouldn't it have been better to tell us that in the first place, and not to have aroused our hopes so fruitlessly?

TONI. After the things you have told me about each other, what did you expect? You know, Douglas, Francis said you tried to murder me. (*A step towards* DOUGLAS.)

DOUGLAS. Dear me.

TONI. (*A step towards* FRANCIS.) And you know, Francis, that Douglas warned me not to marry you.

FRANCIS. How could he!

DOUGLAS. It is lucky that the two of us are not malicious men, or we would be at each other's throats.

TONI. I thought you were.

FRANCIS. Does this interest you? (*He hands her the account.*)

TONI. Where did you find it?

FRANCIS. Does that matter? We are sorry about this, Toni, in a way.

DOUGLAS. (*Closing in on* TONI.) Yes, in a way. But you realise now it's you or us . . . and you so very nearly won. (*There is a knocking on* HARRIS'S *door,* D. L.)

FRANCIS. Who's there?

HARRIS. It's me, sir. I can't get in.

DOUGLAS. The door has jammed, Harris. Go and stay in the pantry till we call for you.

TONI. Harris! Quickly! (DOUGLAS *throws a hand over her mouth.*)

HARRIS. (*Off.*) What was that, miss?

FRANCIS. Miss Oberon asked you to be careful not to damage the door.

HARRIS. Very good, sir. (*They wait, listening.*)

FRANCIS. He's gone. (DOUGLAS *lets* TONI *free.*)

TONI. What are you going to do?

DOUGLAS. It will be as quick a death as one could hope for.

TONI. Tell me what it is.

DOUGLAS. It will only frighten you.

TONI. I'll be brave.

FRANCIS. I'm sure she will, Douglas. Tell us.

DOUGLAS. You remember that dreadful accident that happened in Mother's day to her elder sister, Aunt Estella?

FRANCIS. Oh, no. Not that!

DOUGLAS. Aunt Estella was known to be interested in the torture chamber. So is Cousin Toni.

TONI. What is it?

DOUGLAS. It is a very appropriate mechanism for you, Toni. A little contraption of mediaeval date called the iron maiden, a spring trap with a vicious kiss from whose embrace neither man nor maid may escape.

TONI. Don't you think it is too much of a coincidence for two people to die in it? First your Aunt Estella, and then . . .

FRANCIS. That was a very long time ago.

TONI. What is it you want from me?

FRANCIS. We want our birthright, Toni: our house, our lands, our wealth. We want our own, which you have taken away.

TONI. My dear cousins! Why didn't you ask me for it? I'll give it back to you.

DOUGLAS. You cannot sign this particular inheritance away. There is only one way we can get it back.

FRANCIS. You don't mind if I stay here, Douglas? The sight of those wretched dungeons always sickens me.

DOUGLAS. Stay by all means. This way. (*He begins to lead her towards the cellar opening.*)

TONI. What a pity the Oberons should all come to a dismal end.

FRANCIS. Don't be perturbed on the family's account, Toni. We shall still be here.

TONI. Oh, no.

FRANCIS. What makes you think that?

TONI. Miss Richards is on her way to London. She carries an appeal for help; information about a chemist's bill; and a copy of this photograph. If anything happened to me, do you think you could survive all these?

DOUGLAS. You enlisted that woman's aid! Involving a stranger!

TONI. The odds were against me.

DOUGLAS. What an outrageous thing to do. Francis, as a matter of principle we ought to carry out our plan, and risk the consequences.

TONI. There is no risk, Douglas, it's a certainty. If I go, you go, and no more Oberons.

FRANCIS. No Oberons! That's unthinkable.

TONI. I agree, and when they get my message the police will soon be here.

DOUGLAS. You shouldn't have asked for outside help.

TONI. The traditional feminine weakness, Douglas. As you said, it had to be one of us, and you so very nearly won.

FRANCIS. Congratulations, cousin, on a well-judged race. You cut it a little fine at the finish.

DOUGLAS. Is this the finish, Francis?

FRANCIS. I can see it coming, Douglas. The evidence is there.

DOUGLAS. We could still even off the score.

FRANCIS. What's the use, brother? Circumstances are too obviously against us. We are marked. Information is dispersed. We do not improve the situation by putting Toni out of the way.

DOUGLAS. We might chase after that other woman.

FRANCIS. Small fry, Douglas. Let us not demean ourselves.

DOUGLAS. As you say, Francis. So sorry that we should have ended your visit on such an alarming note.

TONI. I quite understand.

DOUGLAS. You realise that it had to be you or us? And here's your wrap, your gloves . . . (*Moving to collect her things from* D. L.)

FRANCIS. Your case. (*Getting it from* R. *They are very solicitous to see that she has all her things. It might be the finish of a lovely weekend to see the three of them together.*)

DOUGLAS. Is this all you're taking?

TONI. Most of my things I'm leaving here.

FRANCIS. I'll ring for Harris. (*He is about to pull bell-pull.*) Oh, I forgot. (*He unlocks door and calls* "Harris, Harris" *through doorway.*)

TONI. How sweet of you. What a shame I have to leave. Things might have been so different.

DOUGLAS. Things are what they must be. There is no changing or effacing them. I never guessed you would make such opposition. Tell me, how was it you always knew our next step in advance?

TONI. You did exactly what I should have done myself. (*Enter* HARRIS, D. L.)

FRANCIS. Miss Oberon is leaving.

HARRIS. Yes, sir.

FRANCIS. Put this bag in the back of the car.

HARRIS. Very good, sir. (*Takes bag and goes out* U. R.)

FRANCIS. We will not embarrass you by prolonging this parting. All that needs to be said has been said. The important things remain, as always, unvoiced.

DOUGLAS. Our regards to Miss Richards. One day she may realise all she has meant to us.

TONI. I have enjoyed my stay. Oh, I almost forgot to give you this. (*Moving down to them.*)

DOUGLAS. What is it?

FRANCIS. (*Reading the scrap of paper* TONI *has given him.*) "Marriage or murder." It's the scrap of paper on which we planned our little episode.

DOUGLAS. When did you find this?

TONI. The evening I arrived.

DOUGLAS. You wouldn't like to join us in a final drink?

TONI. I'd rather not. Don't let me stop you having yours. Good-bye, Francis, Douglas, good-bye. (*Exit U. R.*)

DOUGLAS. She knew.

FRANCIS. Apparently.

DOUGLAS. Remarkable girl. Tradition will not die as long as she lives here. (*Pause.*) The police are on their way.

FRANCIS. I think our final toast might be in deep appreciation of the girl.

DOUGLAS. I quite agree. (*As of one accord they go to the side-board, pick up their respective decanters, take them back to their places at table and pour out their drinks, standing in their original positions at table.*) Here's to Cousin Toni. (*They raise their glasses as* HARRIS *enters U. R.*)

HARRIS. I wouldn't drink that, sir, if I were you.

DOUGLAS. Why not?

HARRIS. It's poisoned, sir. And I wouldn't drink that either, sir, if I were you.

FRANCIS. Why not, Harris? Is it poisoned, too?

HARRIS. I fancy so.

DOUGLAS. Don't be idiotic, Harris. Who would do such a thing?

HARRIS. Your brother, sir.

DOUGLAS. Harris, I would die rather than believe that.

FRANCIS. And who would poison my drink, Harris?

HARRIS. Your brother, sir.

FRANCIS. That is a contradiction in terms, Harris. My

brother is my brother, we are indivisible. It would be as illogical to poison myself as to poison him.

HARRIS. As you say, sir, but there is strychnine in the one glass and arsenic in the other.

DOUGLAS. Did you see it done, Harris?

HARRIS. No, sir. But I have a presupposition.

DOUGLAS. If you must have intuitions, Harris, keep them to yourself. Besides, what else is there? You said the general public did not like to see their heroes finish at the rope's end.

HARRIS. It seems a pity, sir.

FRANCIS. Let us have no snivelling sentiment at the last moment, Harris. What would you have us do? Face the indignity of investigation? The public horror, the mundane curiosity: provide the proletariat with excitement, entertain the vulgar middle-classes?

HARRIS. Perhaps not, sir. (*Moves D. L.*)

FRANCIS. Besides, Harris, so little is done nowadays in the grand manner. We have lost everything else. Leave us our flourish.

HARRIS. Will that be all, sir?

DOUGLAS. That will be all, Harris. (*There is something very final about that* "all." HARRIS *bows and goes out D. L.*) To Cousin Toni.

FRANCIS. To Cousin Toni.

(*They stand to toast her, hold their glasses up a fraction of a second; then, most unostentatiously, they drink . . . and as they drink:*)

THE CURTAIN FALLS

PROPERTY PLOT

ACT ONE—SCENE ONE

On Stage:
Easy chairs
Stool
Sofa
Sideboard
Ancient weapons on walls
Oil portraits on walls
Book shelves with bound
    leather volumes
Bell-pull
Flower vase or bowl
Dining table and chairs
Dining table set for dinner
    with goblets, tumblers, letter
    in envelope, walnuts in silver
    dish

Personal:

HARRIS:
    Port and brandy on tray
    (*off* L.)

Personal:

FRANCIS:
    Photographs in wallet

TONI:
    Fur cape, luggage, etc.

MISS RICHARDS:
    Camera fitted with flash
        device, handbag, note-book
        and pencil

DOUGLAS:
    Large coloured silk
        handkerchief

Effects (off):
Front door bell (twice)
Clock chiming the quarter
Heaving and dragging noise
    from cellar
Car in the drive
Car lights going past windows

ACT ONE—SCENE TWO

Set:
    Silver, swords and cleaning
        materials on table

Personal:

MISS RICHARDS
    Camera

Effects (off):
Front door bell
Cousin Toni singing
Clock chiming and striking
    noon
Crash of falling masonry in
    cellar (twice)

ACT TWO—SCENE ONE

Personal:
FRANCIS:
    Book

DOUGLAS:
    Invalid chair (*off* D.L.)
    He wears a scarf

91

Personal:

MISS RICHARDS:
  Bag containing papers
  Camera

TONI:
  Book (*on sofa*)

Effects (off):
Front door bell
Clock strikes
On sideboard:
  A pineapple and knife on a
  plate

ACT TWO—SCENE TWO

Personal:

TONI:

  Flowers; twigs of blossom

HARRIS:

  Paper packets (two)
  Silver tray set with tea for
  two (two teapots), lemon,
  sugar and petits fours.

Personal:

DOUGLAS:

  A walking stick
  A parcel, tied and stamped

(*off*):

Letters and parcels U.R. in hall

ACT III

Set:
Table set for dinner
MS. on mantelpiece
Camera on sideboard
Handbag on sideboard:
  In it, photo and scroll of
  paper
Decanters on sideboard

Personal:

HARRIS:
  Port and brandy on tray
  Coffee on tray. (D.L.)

Effects (off):
Front door bell
Sound of bolting a heavy door
  beyond Harris's exit D.L.

DOUGLAS:
  Packet of poison

HARRIS:
  Packet of poison

TONI:
  Suitcase, wraps, gloves, etc.

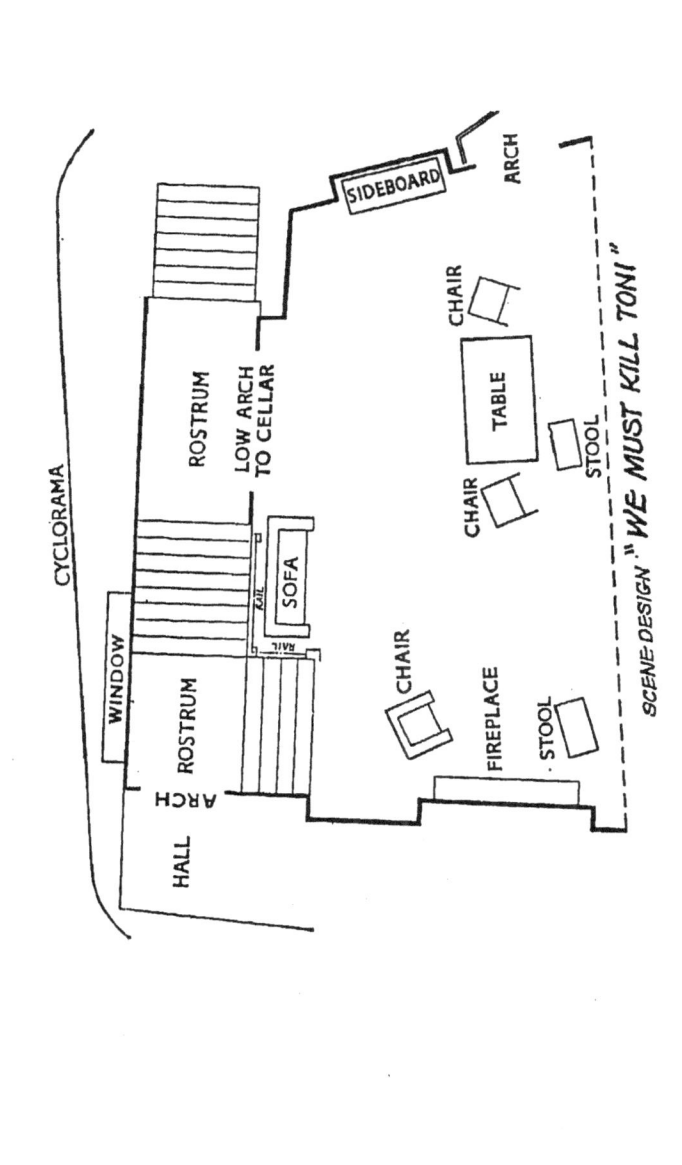

SCENE DESIGN "WE MUST KILL TONI"

NO SEX PLEASE, WE'RE BRITISH
Anthony Marriott and Alistair Foot

Farce / 7 m, 3 f / Interior

A young bride who lives above a bank with her husband who is the assistant manager, innocently sends a mail order off for some Scandinavian glassware. What comes is Scandinavian pornography. The plot revolves around what is to be done with the veritable floods of pornography, photographs, books, films and eventually girls that threaten to engulf this happy couple. The matter is considerably complicated by the man's mother, his boss, a visiting bank inspector, a police superintendent and a muddled friend who does everything wrong in his reluctant efforts to set everything right, all of which works up to a hilarious ending of closed or slamming doors. This farce ran in London over eight years and also delighted Broadway audiences.

"Titillating and topical."
– NBC TV

"A really funny Broadway show."
– ABC TV

COCKEYED
William Missouri Downs

Comedy / 3m, 1f / Unit Set

Phil, an average nice guy, is madly in love with the beautiful Sophia. The only problem is that she's unaware of his existence. He tries to introduce himself but she looks right through him. When Phil discovers Sophia has a glass eye, he thinks that might be the problem, but soon realizes that she really can't see him. Perhaps he is caught in a philosophical hyperspace or dualistic reality or perhaps beautiful women are just unaware of nice guys. Armed only with a B.A. in philosophy, Phil sets out to prove his existence and win Sophia's heart. This fast moving farce is the winner of the HotCity Theatre's GreenHouse New Play Festival. The St. Louis Post-Dispatch called Cockeyed a clever romantic comedy, Talkin' Broadway called it "hilarious," while Playback Magazine said that it was "fresh and invigorating."

Winner!
of the HotCity Theatre GreenHouse New Play Festival

"Rocking with laughter...hilarious...polished and engaging work draws heavily on the age-old conventions of farce: improbable situations, exaggerated characters, amazing coincidences, absurd misunderstandings, people hiding in closets and barely missing each other as they run in and out of doors...full of comic momentum as Cockeyed hurtles toward its conclusion."
–Talkin' Broadway

www.ingramcontent.com/pod-product-compliance
Lightning Source LLC
Chambersburg PA
CBHW070636120726
47909CB00004B/1462